Royal House of Leone

The KING'S
BOUGHT
BRIDE

by Jennifer Lewis

1

"How can I possibly choose a wife in only thirty days?" Darias Leone suppressed a curse as he pushed open the tall, heavy door and entered the New York art gallery hosting his new show. It was almost dark outside, and he blinked in the bright light of the gallery space. He was under so much pressure right now he could barely focus on his own paintings. "That old edict is ridiculous."

His brother Sandro exhaled. "It's only twenty-five days now. They count the days since the last monarch died. And you know how Mom is about tradition. She's already devastated by the loss of her husband. You don't want to stress her by pushing for reforms to a thousand-year-old law."

"I don't. But I also don't want to get stuck with some snooty Austrian 'princess' that she's dug up for me. This is the rest of my life we're talking about." He strode toward the biggest painting. The light wasn't hitting it right.

"You could always divorce her. There's some loophole from the eighteenth century about one year being enough."

"And spark a six-hundred-year feud? I don't think so. If I marry another European monarch, I'll have to stick with her for life."

"So marry someone else. An American. What about your last girlfriend—the model?"

Darias grunted. "Are you kidding? She'd probably turn a divorce into a three-ring circus that would leave her ruling half of Altaleone."

"Good point. You'd need an ironclad prenup."

"And what kind of girl wants to start a marriage like that?" The situation was impossible. "Even if I did have one in mind. Which I totally don't." He looked around the gallery for Keane Moss, the owner. Not seeing him, he strode toward the front desk. "The angles on the spotlights are wrong. They're throwing the brushstrokes into relief and distracting from the image."

The girl behind the desk looked up from her phone. "Sorry?"

"Where's Keane?"

"He'll be here in about twenty minutes. Can I help you with something?"

"No, thanks. I'll wait." He walked back to Sandro. "You can leave if you want. I have to get this fixed."

"What about her?" Sandro glanced over Darias's shoulder.

Darias turned. He didn't see anyone but the girl at the desk. "What about her? What are you talking about?"

Sandro stepped closer and spoke with a hushed voice. "What about asking *her* to marry you?"

"Are you mad? I don't even know her name. She's not the usual girl."

"She looks the part."

Darias turned again. She looked like every other

gallery assistant in New York: tall, willowy, beautiful in a generic way. "Looks aren't everything, you know."

"You could offer her money, a detailed contract spelling out everything you'd require of her for one year. Then after the last day of that year you go your separate ways."

"Maybe she doesn't need money." This was the dumbest idea he'd ever heard.

"Everyone needs money, Darias. It's just a question of how much. Think about it. What the heck else are you going to do?"

Darias narrowed his eyes. Was this girl mercenary enough to accept such a proposal? Her long blonde hair was tied back in a neat ponytail, and she wore no jewelry and little makeup on her admittedly very pretty face. She looked far too sensible to accept such a proposal. And she was tapping away on her phone again. "We'd need a clause about how she can't do that during royal dinners."

Sandro laughed. And so did Darias. She looked up and her gaze startled him—gray-green and haunting. She put her phone away with a guilty look.

"Don't mind us," said Sandro. "He's the artist."

"Of course. I know that." She stood quickly and held out her hand and shook Darias's. "Emma Ricci. I'm only here three evenings a week."

"What do you do the rest of the time?" asked Sandro as she shook his hand.

"I'm a teacher. Elementary school, but school's out for the summer so I'm doing some temping as well."

Darias could feel Sandro's eyes on him. Probably thinking about how "nice" and suitable she was. How did he know she wasn't a porn star on weekends?

Sandro started tapping away on his phone. Probably googling her name. His brother loved to leap into a thing.

Her phone pinged. "Do excuse me." She frowned as she read the text, then bit her lip—which was disturbingly full and pink. "I know this is going to sound terrible, but—" She hesitated.

Darias lifted a brow. "What? I'm intrigued."

"Would you mind if I ran out for a minute? Just to the bank on the corner. Since you're the artist I know I can trust you."

"I do hope so," said Darias archly. "But sure. If Keane comes I'll tell him I sent you somewhere. That's the kind of obnoxious behavior he expects of a European royal." He smiled warmly.

She darted out the door, hair flying, before he had time to change his mind.

"Probably just stepped out to buy some crack," he teased Sandro, as the heavy glass door closed behind her. "Or sell it."

"Nonsense. Keane would get a full background check on his employees before putting them in charge of all this valuable art. Hey, I found her Facebook." His face softened into a smile. "She's posted all these cute animal pictures. "

Darias peered at the screen, which contained a pretty picture of her with the sun in her hair. "She only has twenty-three friends. And she should know better than to leave her privacy settings wide open. This page probably a front."

"The average person doesn't have thousands of friends, and isn't expecting to be stalked by the press. Besides, you should know by now that I'm an excellent judge of character." Sandro snatched his phone back and tapped some more. "Aww, look at her Twitter feed. It's full of inspirational quotes." He tugged his brother's arm. "Here's one from Mother Theresa."

Darias laughed. "And on the strength of that you think I should ask her to marry me?"

"Do you have any better ideas?"

"Darias!" Keane Moss burst through the door, silver hair bouncing, clipped British accent in force. "We were all shocked by the news. How was the funeral?"

"Sad." Darias had been asked this question at least ten times today alone. His answer was growing rude. "But all went smoothly, so I'm grateful for that."

Keane glanced at the empty desk. "What have you two scoundrels done with my gallery assistant?"

"I sent her out to run an errand for me," said Darias quickly, before Sandro could respond. "Sorry. She'll be back in a moment."

He felt Sandro shoot him a sideways glance.

"Royal arrogance!" Keane smiled and shook his head. "Irresistible, I'm sure. How do you like the way we hung the show?"

Darias launched into a litany of complaints about the spotlights and pointed out three paintings that needed to be rehung on the same wall as they were a triptych of sorts. He was about to suggest raising another painting higher when the door opened and the girl came back. She froze when she saw her boss standing there.

"I told Keane I'd sent you to run an errand for me," Darias said with a deadpan expression. "I do appreciate it. Did it go as planned?"

"Uh, yes. Just as planned." She blinked, looking confused.

"Thank you."

"You're welcome." She looked from one to the other, obviously trying to figure out what was going on. "Mr. Moss, there are some messages on the desk in your office."

"Thanks, love. I'll get onto the boys about fixing the lights while I'm in there. Back in a mo."

Keane loped off toward his office. "Now's your chance," hissed Sandro, before he moved off to the furthest corner of the gallery.

Darias walked slowly over to the girl at the desk. She'd pulled out her ponytail band and her long blonde hair hung over her face as she tapped into her phone again. She looked up as he approached. "Thank you for covering for me."

"What were you doing at the bank?" asked Darias. Why beat about the bush?

She flushed. "I had to transfer some money to my brother."

"In such a rush that you had to abandon your desk?"

"He's in some...trouble." She glanced about. "He borrowed money from the wrong people and I had to get it to him right away."

"A lot of money?"

She nodded. Her pretty face was drawn and she looked like she was about to cry.

Sandro might well be onto something. "I have a

proposal."

Emma shrank into her chair. It was nice of him to make an excuse so she didn't get fired, but she didn't intend to return his favor with a sexual one. He probably had no idea that she was propositioned by half the men who walked into the gallery. Especially the artists. They had the biggest egos. "Oh?"

Darias Leone—the gallery's most overpriced artist and a wealthy European royal to boot—towered over her desk. "I need a wife."

She had no response to that. Her phone pinged with the arrival of a text.

His dark eyes flashed. "Go ahead. Check it."

She did. Her brother saying thanks with a lot of exclamation points. Jesus. Fourteen hundred dollars? The amount got bigger each time. She'd just given him her rent money. Thank goodness she had this second job. Temping was great when you had a steady gig but she'd only worked two days last week. "My brother. Problem solved." She managed a shaky smile. "Thanks again."

"You need money." It wasn't a question.

She shrugged. "Who doesn't?"

"You need money; I need a wife for one year. It would be a purely business arrangement, totally secret. You'd play the part, I'd pay you handsomely, and at the end of that year we'd part amicably and no one would ever know the truth."

She blinked. Her heart pounded, and she wasn't sure if it was from the sheer madness of the proposal he'd just hurled at her or the fierce stare that pinned her to her chair while he made it. She scrambled for a response. "Won't you have to live overseas?"

"Altaleone. It's in the Alps just north of Italy. I'm to be king. At least if I can find a wife in less than thirty days."

She knew most of this already. The daytime gallery assistant had clued her in with all the gossipy details about Darias while exclaiming over how hot he was. "I can't imagine it would be so hard to find a wife. You're very handsome, successful"—she gestured to the gallery, which displayed nearly three million dollars in potential sales of his work—"and royal. I think you need to talk to the Millionaire Matchmaker."

"I need things simple. Cut and dried."

"But you don't know me at all. What if I'm crazy?" She lifted a brow and widened her eyes as if to suggest it might be a possibility.

"My brother prides himself on being a great judge of character and he's already vouched for you." Now a smile tugged at the corner of his mouth. "Meet me for a drink after your shift. What time do you get off?"

She stiffened. This was the kind of proposal she'd grown used to. He probably just wanted to promise her the moon and get her in the sack, then dump her. "I don't think so."

"Emma! Can you come back here a moment?" Keane's voice called from the back of the gallery.

"Excuse me." She scurried off, relieved to escape his punishing gaze. Keane took off his reading glasses as she entered. He hated being seen in them. "Darling, can you take Darias and his brother out to Lucci's and buy them dinner for me?" He stuck out his business credit card. "I want them out of here while the show is rehung, or he'll micromanage every detail and we'll never get it done. The photographer from *Art World* is coming first thing tomorrow so I don't have time for fussing."

She gulped. "What about the front desk?"

"The show's not open yet, so never mind the front desk. Quickly, please. Dan and Aziz will be here any minute."

"Uh, okay." *Really?* At least she'd get a free dinner out of it. And it wasn't as if he could *make* her marry him. How bad could it be?

2

Not surprisingly, Emma had no trouble convincing the brothers to eat out with her. While they walked the two blocks to the restaurant, she wondered silently what else she could do in the evenings to supplement her meager teacher's income when she got fired from this job. She knew Keane had hired her entirely for her looks, but this was ridiculous. Was he going to blame her if she made their biggest client angry by refusing to marry him?

"Why did your brother borrow money?" Darias watched the waiter fill their glasses with red wine. His brother Sandro pored over the menu.

Emma hesitated. This was her personal business. On the other hand…"Drugs. He's an addict." Perfect, really. He'd hardly want a royal wife with a junkie brother.

To her surprise, his eyes filled with compassion. "You probably aren't helping him by funding his habit.

"I know, but what am I supposed to do? Let him get his kneecaps broken?"

"Sometimes people have to hit bottom before they can find their way back up again."

She shuddered. "I'm trying to make sure he doesn't hit bottom too hard. He's the only family I have left. If I could just convince him to go to rehab.…" She took a sip of wine, then regretted it when the acrid taste burned her tongue.

His eyes brightened. "I know the owner of the best rehab in the city. The Fountains. We could book him in today."

"We? You don't even know him." This man was too much.

"It's perfect, don't you see? Your brother goes to The Fountains—which is very expensive, and I will pay every penny—and you come to Altaleone for a year. In a year's time, your brother will be clean and sober, and you can come back to New York with a nice big bank account and start over."

"It's an excellent plan," said Sandro, who was almost as annoyingly good-looking and self-confident as Darias. "And I can vouch for Darias. He's a man of his word in every way."

"Except that he's planning to live a lie for a solid year." She looked right at Darias while she said it. "Is that really how you want to start your reign as king?"

His brows lowered slightly. "Of course not, but my main concern right now is helping my mother through a terrible shock. Altaleone is a very small country. You'd have few public appearances and official duties. The year would be over before you know it."

"I have a career!" she protested. "I spent years working for my degree, and I'm finally a teacher. I love my work. I don't want to leave it to go live in some fantasy fairy tale for a year."

Sandro laughed. "A lot of people would love the chance to live in a fantasy fairy tale."

"Not me. If things look too good to be true, they scare the hell out of me. I was thrilled that my brother hadn't asked me for money for six whole weeks. Turns out he was borrowing it from the mob."

Darias cocked his head slightly. "The Fountains has a ninety percent success rate. I don't think anywhere boasts better results."

She'd heard of The Fountains. Of course it had never crossed her mind that she'd be able to afford to send Jonas there. Not that he'd agree to go, of course.

Darias leaned toward her, fixing her with his dark stare. "Do you want to look back a few years from now and realize that you had a chance to send your brother to the best rehab facility in the world, and you turned it down?"

She swallowed. He had a point. "But I don't know anything about pretending to be queen. I'm from South Orange, New Jersey. I barely know which fork to use." She gestured at the forks on the white tablecloth.

Darias snorted. "That stuff is easy. You can pick it up in an afternoon. It sounds crude, but you look the part and that probably is more important than anything."

Her back stiffened as his eyes traveled over her face and neck. "Won't they be expecting you to marry an aristocrat?"

He shrugged. "Beauty trumps titles. And even royal families aren't as old fashioned as they used to be. Look at William and Kate in England. She's not an aristocrat."

Emma felt her chest grow tighter. "One year exactly?" Twelve months. Was it really that long? "And you'd pay for my brother to stay at The Fountains for that entire time?"

"As long as he needs to be there. And I'd pay you one hundred thousand dollars up front on the signing of the contract, to do whatever you like with, and another hundred thousand at the end of the year. In the meantime, all your expenses will be taken care of and you'll have a generous allowance for clothing, entertainment, anything you want."

She felt ill. Was she seriously considering this? From what she'd read and heard about Darias he seemed like a decent guy. Heck, a lot of women would probably kill for this opportunity. A hundred thousand dollars was a lot of money. It would take her years to save that much at her job. Not that she could ever manage to save anything with Jonas borrowing and wasting every cent she earned. And she'd be getting two hundred thousand in total—and living for free for an entire year.

And Jonas—if he could get off drugs it would transform both of their lives.

"You'd have to keep it a secret from everyone, even your parents." Darias looked so calm. "You'd never be able to tell them the truth."

"My parents are both gone." It was hard to say, even now, when her mom had been dead almost a year. "My brother is my family. I couldn't tell him the truth either?"

"You could just tell him that you fell madly in love with me." The twinkle in his eyes showed that he found the situation amusing. "Do you think he'd find that hard to imagine?"

She looked at Darias, gorgeous, rich, royal and dangerously charming. "No. But what if he won't go into rehab? I couldn't leave unless he was safely there."

"I'll talk to Licia, my friend who owns it. I'm sure she'll have a solution. They kidnapped Katie Reese when she was at her lowest, and now she's up for a Tony. I know they pride themselves on working miracles."

Emma let out a long, slow breath. One year. Three hundred and sixty-five days. She'd survived hard times for a lot longer than that.

"You're thinking about it." Darias looked pleased. The waitress came over, and he shocked her by ordering for all three of them—in Italian. "I didn't want you to be distracted by another decision. Trust me, I will take care of your every need during this one year."

"That's a big promise." How did he know what "needs" she would have? She certainly didn't.

"I don't shirk my commitments. That's why I need a wife on short notice. Do you think I really want to leave New York City and go live in an ancient castle? It's my duty. You can trust me to do my duty to you."

"You don't even know if I'm crazy."

"Are you crazy?" He didn't look that worried.

"Aren't we all deep down? I mean, why does a wealthy prince feel the need to make art? That seems rather eccentric."

He laughed. "I suppose I prefer to think of myself as creative, but eccentric will do. Do you have any eccentricities?"

"I don't have time for eccentricities. I work full-time teaching fourth graders, then I work at the gallery three evenings a week. If I can buy groceries, keep my apartment clean and catch a few moments to escape into a book, I count myself lucky."

"In Altaleone you'd have time to pursue your interests."

"I'm not even sure I have any interests." She didn't want him getting the idea that she was some kind of mysterious damsel with hidden depths.

"Maybe you've just never had the luxury of enough time and resources to find out."

The waiter bought their food, a gleaming slice of meat among brightly colored vegetables, with a side of pasta in fragrant pesto. Her stomach growled. She'd only had time for a granola bar at lunch. "This looks wonderful. But what if I was vegetarian? You didn't even ask."

He frowned slightly. "If you were vegetarian, surely you'd have told me."

"Are you kidding? I'd be too intimidated."

"Nonsense. You radiate a quiet confidence that can be seen for miles. Doesn't she, Sandro?"

Sandro looked up from his plate and nodded in agreement. "You already look like a queen, too. That goes a long way."

Emma frowned. "What does a queen look like? I'm picturing an elderly lady with a bouffant hairdo and a Hermès scarf."

"That does sound somewhat like my grandmother Queen Sofia." His dark eyes filled with sadness. "Who died a few days ago. But my brother means that you are naturally regal in the way you carry yourself. You are tall, with strong but elegant bone structure and the kind of beauty that has inspired artists throughout the ages."

He spoke softly, and his words had the effect of making heat rise to her cheeks. Which was just annoying! People had been telling her for years that she was pretty, but that didn't butter any biscuits where she came from. All it did was invite unwelcome attention from unsuitable men. She downplayed it by never wearing makeup and keeping her hair in a ponytail most of the time. "I guess I should thank you for the compliment. But how come you're the heir? You've mentioned your mother. Why doesn't she inherit?"

"My father would have been the one to inherit. He was next in the royal line, and in the event of his death the crown passes to the next blood relative in the Leone line—me. My father was found dead on the same night as my grandmother. Don't you watch the news?"

"No. I don't have time. I figure if a war breaks out someone will tell me. What happened?"

"No one knows exactly." His face darkened. "My grandmother was suffocated. My father was stabbed through the heart with an ancient dagger."

Her eyes widened. "They were murdered."

"It appears so, though some are saying it was part of a ritual. The circumstances are…mysterious. The police are still analyzing the evidence."

"That's horrible. And sounds dangerous. Are you worried they'll try to kill you, too?"

"I find worry to be a waste of time. Perhaps for the same reasons you don't bother to watch the news. Why give energy to something that isn't important to you? I do, however, intend to find out exactly what happened and who is responsible. Every moment I spend in New York is time where the trail grows cold."

"Then why are you here?"

"I have a commitment to Keane Moss. He's represented my paintings for five years, and I owe him a lot. I'm here to open this show, which has been in the works for over a year, and then I'll be leaving." He paused and his gaze trapped hers. Then he reached across the table. Her skin stung with awareness as he wrapped his fingers around her hand, which had been resting by her water glass. "And I sincerely hope that you'll come with me."

Her phone pinged. "Excuse me." She was glad of an excuse to snatch her hand back. Already her heart beat faster and her breathing grew shallow. She pulled her phone from her purse and her heart flew to her mouth when she saw Jonas's name next to an all-caps message.

NEED MORE $. FORGOT ABOUT INTEREST. HAVE UNTIL TOMORROW. CALL ME ASAP. LOVE YOU.

Her heart sank. There seemed to be no end to the trouble her brother could get into. And she'd already have to wait for her next paycheck just to make her rent. People said she should serve him some tough love, but how did she do that when he was all she had? "One hundred thousand, up front, you said."

"Yes." His eyes brightened. "And another at the close of the year."

"How can you be sure The Fountains will take my brother?"

"Let me call Licia." He whipped out his phone, explained the situation, and booked Jonas in—starting tomorrow at nine A.M., without even consulting her. Then he hung up and pocketed his phone. "It's all arranged." The tiniest hint of a smile tugged at his arrogant mouth.

Her brother at The Fountains tomorrow morning. This could be the big break that turned everything around for him. She'd have enough to pay off whatever stupid debts he'd racked up and money to save. She could put her stuff into storage for a year and give up her apartment, which was drafty and noisy, anyway…. "I'd need to see the contract. The one between us."

He pulled his phone out again and pushed a button. "Greg, can we meet tonight?" He explained the situation to his lawyer and made plans for them to head straight to his office, despite the late hour.

She wanted to protest that she should go back to the gallery first, but Keane probably needed her to keep Darias away until the show was rehung, which might take another hour or two.

She swallowed hard. One year. And it wasn't like she'd be in prison. She'd get to see another part of the world. "I've never even left the U.S." It felt important to make it clear to him that she was not as sophisticated as she apparently appeared.

"Then it's about time you did." He paid the bill with an air of satisfaction. "The gallery opening is tomorrow night, and we can leave for Altaleone first thing in the morning."

They split from Sandro, and Darias drove her to his lawyer's midtown office in his big Mercedes G-Class SUV. Already she felt like she was being whisked off to…something. Riding up in the mirrored elevator, she felt self-conscious—dressed like a kid in the black jeans, black T-shirt and black Converse sneakers that were her unofficial uniform at the gallery. Darias wasn't formally dressed, but expensive Italian designer casual was a whole different groove.

The young lawyer maintained a poker face as Darias described his outrageous plan. He did take a good long look at Emma, though, and she felt as if her skin might peel right off under his cold, analytical gaze. "It'll take me an hour or so to research a couple of matters and get something typed up."

Darias took her to a nearby bar, where she stuck strictly to plain tonic water. She was a lightweight at the best of times and wanted to read—and sign—the contract with a clear head. Her brother had called her three times and left messages while they were in with the lawyer, and she finally called him back.

3

"Jesus, Emma! Why are you ignoring me?" Jonas sounded jittery and panicked over the phone, as usual.

She glanced around to make sure no one in the bar was staring, then no attempt to hide her exasperation from her voice. "I sent you fourteen hundred dollars tonight, Jonas. And now you say that isn't enough! Or are you calling because you're ready to pay me back?"

"This is serious! These guys are the real deal. I paid back what I borrowed, but they want another eight hundred. Can't you sell Mom's engagement ring?"

"I already pawned it two months ago. Do you think I'm made of money?" It had half killed her to see her mom's modest ring go, but then her parents had never actually been married, so how much did it mean? And she knew her mom would want her to help Jonas. "But listen, I have a plan. Are you at home?"

"Yeah." He lived in a walkup in Hell's Kitchen with two other wannabe actors. They weren't all that far from there right now.

"I can give you all the money you need to pay

back the debt, on one condition—"

Darias grabbed her hand, startling her and making her look up at him. He held a finger to his lips, reminding her to keep their whole plan secret. She nodded.

"I'll give you the money tonight if you agree to go into rehab at The Fountains tomorrow morning at nine A.M. You'll have to stay with me all night, though, because I don't trust you not to disappear." It hurt to be so cold to him, but she'd been burned before.

"The Fountains costs a fricken fortune, sis. Did you win the lotto?"

How could she explain this? Presumably, the whole world would soon know she was marrying Darias. But until she'd seen and signed the contract, she didn't want to let any cats out of bags. "I have something going on in my life, Jonas, that I haven't told you about yet. I'll tell you tonight, if you'll stay with me, then go to The Fountains."

"Are you messing with me?"

"I'm not. You have to take this seriously." She wanted to tell him that this could be his last chance to turn his life around, but Jonas didn't respond well to pressure. "They're professionals who help people with addictions all day long, but you have to commit." If he didn't, there would be no point in going along with Darias's wild plan. "Things keep getting worse and worse for you. I'm worried you're going to wind up dead."

"I tried to quit. But then Danny came over and…"

"At The Fountains you'd be away from all the

people who'd try to drag you under. It's a chance to get your life back."

She could almost hear him thinking, while tapping his fingers nervously on something, the way he did when he was strung out. "Okay. Deal. I'll do it if I can get the money tonight."

"And I'm coming with you to drop it off."

"No way, sis. These dudes are heavy. You don't want to go anywhere near them."

Darias took her hand again, and she looked up. "I'll go with him," he mouthed.

Her eyes widened. "We'll figure it out. I'll call you within the hour. Stay home. Don't go anywhere or do anything until you hear from me." She hung up.

Darias lifted a brow. "I overheard. Of course you can't go with him."

"And you can?"

He shrugged. "I have security."

Forty-five minutes later she was inking her name to a surprisingly short contract in which she agreed to be the legal wife of Darias Xavier Augustin Leone of Altaleone, and to perform all offices required to convince both family and the public that there was indeed a legitimate and loving union for the period of one year and one month. (The lawyer had pointed out that the year couldn't start until after the wedding—which would take place in Altaleone—and Darias had thrown in another fifty thousand dollars for the extra month or so that would require.) She was pledged to absolute secrecy, both now and forever, and if she broke the contract at any point she'd be legally obliged to return all the money. The first portion would be wired into her account tomorrow as soon as the banks opened.

A single paragraph committed the funds for her brother to remain at The Fountains until such time as she returned to the States, or he was considered by their expert staff to be free of his addiction, whichever came first.

"I feel like I just signed my life away."

"You did." He smiled. "But only for a year. You'll get it back. And I'm deliriously grateful for your sacrifice. Let's go find your brother."

In less than twenty minutes, they were climbing the steps to Jonas's walkup. He opened the door looking harried. "You got the money?" Then he noticed Darias.

"I have a surprise, Jonas. This is Darias." She pushed an attempted smile to her lips. "We're getting married."

"What?" Jonas looked confused for a moment. Then he shoved a hand through his tangled hair and stared at Darias. He thrust his hand out, and Darias shook it.

"Pleased to met you, Jonas." Darias didn't smile.

Jonas stared at her. "Does he...know?"

"About the money? Yes. And he's arranged your stay that The Fountains. I'm very thankful."

Jonas looked doubtful. "You do have it, though, right? The eight hundred. Because they just called again. They want it by nine."

"It's not easy to get that kind of money at night, Jonas," she said. She was so angry with him, and she didn't want to make it too easy. She'd just introduced the man that—for all Jonas knew—

she planned to spend the rest of her life with, and he barely acknowledged him. "My ATM won't give out that much at once."

"Shit." He shoved a hand through his hair again.

"But we have it," said Darias. "Let's go."

Darias had arranged for two members of his personal security staff to tail them to the location. One would go in with Jonas and escort him out again. Darias wanted to go himself, but Emma persuaded him that he might be recognized if news of his family tragedy had been circulating.

By 9:45, Jonas's debt was paid. Darias went home to his loft in Soho, and she went back to Jonas's place to help him pack. One of Darias's security guards stayed outside as a precaution. She told Jonas she'd be living abroad with Darias, and that she'd store his stuff with hers until he needed it. Since he'd sold nearly everything he'd ever owned to buy drugs, his worldly effects fit into three cardboard boxes from the liquor store, and the security guard loaded them into the back of his SUV.

"This is weird, sis. I can tell your new man is loaded. Is he mobbed up?"

"No." At least she didn't think so. She only knew what she'd read in the media like everyone else. "He's from a small country called Altaleone. I'll tell you more about it after I move there." She didn't want to reveal that her future husband was royal. Jonas would find that out soon enough, and it would be better if he was safely in rehab before he considered the enticing financial implications.

She stayed up with him all night—not that she

would have been able to sleep, anyway—then they went out for breakfast at a nearby deli. At five to nine they were climbing the polished white marble steps of The Fountains at an exclusive address on the Upper East Side.

"I feel like they're going to take one look at me and throw me out." Jonas raked a hand through his hair again.

Emma didn't mention that she felt the same way, especially after staying up all night without even taking a shower. "You'll be fine. This is what they do. In a few months you'll be a—"

"Months! What?"

"Fighting addiction takes time. Look at it as a free luxury vacation at a very expensive resort."

They pushed through shiny revolving doors into a gleaming lobby with tall arches and potted palms. "Now that you put it that way...." A smile spread across his crooked mouth.

Her chest filled with emotion. Hopefully, this big break really would help to heal whatever was so broken inside him. "I'll miss you. I hope I'll be able to come visit, but I'm really not sure how easy it will be to fly back here regularly. Call me any time, though. If I can't answer right away, I'll call back when I can." It was weird not having any inkling what her daily routine would be.

They checked him in with just one small bag of clothes, and she watched as her skinny, crazy brother walked off down the hallway, already trying to charm two staffers.

When she turned around with a sigh, she was shocked to see Darias standing there.

4

"Good morning, Emma."

"Uh, hi." She ran a hand over her hair. She wished she'd had time to make herself more presentable before seeing Darias again. He looked devastatingly gorgeous and effortlessly stylish, as usual. "Did you think I'd try to skip town?

A smile tugged at one corner of his broad mouth. She tried to ignore what it did to her insides. Probably just nerves.

"We leave for Altaleone tomorrow. I thought we could get to know each other better before we travel." They headed out the door and down the steps.

"I have a lot to take care of. I need to pack, put my stuff in storage, quit my job...." At least it was the summer so she wasn't leaving her students in a lurch. The school could find a replacement before classes started again in September.

"I can help. I have time to kill before the show opens tonight."

He had to be kidding. "I live in New Jersey. I take the PATH train. It's right across town."

"It'll be much easier if I drive."

Emma was embarrassed by her dingy second-floor apartment, but at least her landlady wasn't home so she didn't have to make awkward introductions. She knew she'd have no trouble getting out of the lease. They'd offered her money to leave early two months ago because they wanted to renovate and rent it for more.

Darias's tall presence made the space look even smaller. "I'll need to pack up everything I'm keeping. The rest I can donate to the Vietnam Veterans. They pick up."

He rolled up the sleeves of his expensively crumpled white shirt, revealing tanned and muscled forearms that made her blink. "Where do I start?"

Was he serious? One way to find out. "I still have the boxes from my last move." She pulled the flattened cardboard out of the back of her coat closet and grabbed a reel of packing tape from her junk drawer. "Perhaps you could put them together for me while you tell me about your family."

"Excellent." He immediately knelt on her hardwood floor and popped a box upright. She liked him more already. "First let me tell you about my mother, because she's the reason I'm marrying you."

"What's her name?"

"Carolina." He pronounced it *Caroleena.* "She married my dad when she was only twenty-two. She's devoted her whole life to our family. I'd do anything for her."

"Obviously."

He looked up and smiled. "She's worth it. And

she's devastated by the loss of my dad. All of her children had finally flown the nest, and she and my dad were looking forward to traveling and spending more time together, and now he's gone. I do hope you'll become friends with her."

"Me, too." Of course it would be awkward having to keep in the back of her mind that at the end of a year she'd be walking away from her new friend with a lifetime of secrets to keep.

"Does she know your father and his mother were murdered?"

"Yes, but we've all agreed to keep quiet about it while the investigation continues. Nothing good will come of fueling media speculation. She was as surprised as the rest of us."

Emma wondered if that was really true. Still, it wasn't her business. "You have siblings."

"Oh, yes. We're scattered about the world right now, but we all come home to Altaleone from time to time. My twin sister, Beatriz, still lives there. She's taking care of my mom right now."

"Twins? You must be very close."

He paused in his work of taping up a box. "We were once." He sighed. "I've spent so much time in New York in recent years that I've been a lousy brother. I must fix that when we return home."

"Wait." She frowned. "If you're twins, how come she's not the heir as well? Were you born first?"

"She was born first, but in a case where there's a male and female heir, the male inherits."

"That's not very fair."

"I agree. But then fair doesn't play a large role in monarchic succession." Humor twinkled in his eyes.

"You're right. If fair was a factor, there'd be an election." At least he was easy to talk to. "Do you guys actually, like, rule the country and the people?"

Now he laughed. "Of course. But there aren't very many of them and due to Altaleone having the highest per capita export of fine champagne and hand-cut diamonds in the world, they're rather wealthy and content. It's a quiet and sleepy country. Honestly, most people with ambitions and big dreams move somewhere else to pursue them."

"Like you did."

"Exactly. I always knew I'd go home one day, but people are long lived in my family and my dad was only sixty. I didn't imagine becoming king for another twenty years or more."

He popped another box open and taped it. She watched his muscular arms at work. This man was a prince—soon to be a king—and he was helping her pack her blender and her bedding and her toaster oven.

It boggled the mind. "I guess I should call my job and tell them I won't be back in the fall." That felt so final. If she quit her job she was really ditching her whole carefully built life and moving to some country she'd barely heard of.

"You can tell them you'll be back the following year, though." He obviously didn't want her to get any ideas that this life change was permanent. He probably thought she'd get pretty comfortable living in a palace.

Maybe she would.

"Why are you laughing?" He lifted a brow.

"Just thinking about how crazy this is. Why did you pick me? I mean, you don't know me. You could have chosen any girl in the city."

"As my brother pointed out, you look the part. And if Keane hired you, you're likely to be intelligent and charming as well as beautiful."

"Really? I'm flattered. I thought he hired me because I was willing to work in the evenings."

"Do you have any idea how many applications he gets for a gallery assistant position? I've seen stacks of them falling off his desk."

"I suppose Keane Moss is one of the hottest galleries right now." Funny. She hadn't realized it was some kind of big honor. Which was probably a good thing. She'd have been too intimidated to apply if she did. She didn't even know much about modern art. She'd just needed the extra money, and it was easy to get there from the PATH train.

She put her dishes into the first box, layering napkins between them. "I guess I should pack all my clothes, since I'll be there for all four seasons."

"Don't worry about that." He glanced quickly at her black jeans and T-shirt. "You'll need a new wardrobe to play the role of queen. We'll go shopping before we leave."

She blinked. "Okay. But what about towels and sheets? I need to put everything in storage today, and we're not leaving until tomorrow morning. What should I do overnight?"

"You can stay with me."

It didn't take long to pack everything in her apartment into twelve cardboard boxes. She packed underwear, makeup, hair products and another basic black outfit into a sports bag—she didn't own a suitcase—then Darias drove her to the local storage place, where she rented a small room at the yearly rate. Somehow that made it sink in. A whole year in a strange place.

"Now we must buy you some clothes." Darias's eyes slid over her body, sending a very strange feeling through her. "Let's go to Barneys."

Once there, he immediately requested a personal shopper and told her that his fiancée required a varied wardrobe for a trip with a number of formal occasions.

He sat in a chair and read something on his phone—or pretended to—while she walked around the store gathering stuff with the shopper. Once she lifted a price tag and gasped audibly when she saw what the simple gray shirt cost.

After that she just nodded her agreement and wondered how Darias would react when he saw the bill.

This was all his idea.

She had a feeling she'd be saying that a lot during the next year.

The shopper handed her one coordinated outfit at a time. The first was a boring pantsuit in a weird camel color she would never have looked twice at, with a dark blue blouse. She donned it swiftly and came out fully expecting to hear laughter, but watched instead as a satisfied smile spread over the elegant woman's lipsticked mouth.

"We'll take it." Darias's voice made her head snap around. He now stood off to one side, regarding her with approval in his eyes.

Emma snuck another glance in the tall mirror in her changing room to see if they were seeing something different from her. The suit had a surprisingly elegant silhouette, and the color combination did something weird to her complexion that made her cheeks glow pink and her hair shine like gold.

Okay.

They had a similar reaction to almost everything she tried on, including a very fitted silver-blue evening gown with a tiny matching bag. One top was too low cut and a pair of shoes had a strap that dug into her ankle; other than those items they bought everything. Darias told her to keep on the last, rather bohemian ensemble—a pair of patterned skinny jeans, worn with boots and a coordinating blouse.

They stopped in the cosmetics department for her to stock up on necessities and get a quick makeover at the Chanel counter.

She never did find out how much it all cost. Darias paid in silence, and his expression showed nothing more than satisfaction with a job well done.

"I think we just spent more than my last year's salary," she murmured, as they stepped out onto Fifth Avenue.

"It's the cost of doing business," he said with a grin. "Being a monarch isn't cheap. And now you have something to wear to the opening tonight."

She froze. "I'm coming? I haven't even told Keane that I'm quitting."

"He'll figure it out soon enough. And it will be the perfect place to announce our engagement.

Just enough press to get the word out, but we won't be mobbed."

Emma sucked in a breath. The idea of announcing their engagement to the world terrified her. It probably would have frightened her even if it wasn't fake.

Which it wasn't. The engagement was real. She really was going to marry him.

She just didn't love him.

"We need to get you a ring. Everyone will be staring at your finger. Let's head to Tiffany."

She snuck a glance at Darias as they drove toward Tiffany to drop a few more thousand on a ring. So gorgeous, warm, charming and generous he seemed like the man of any woman's dreams. But he wasn't, not really. He didn't want to be tied down. That was why they were going through this charade. To make it easy for him to divorce her and move on, with none of that inconvenient "'til death do us part" business.

So she'd better be very, very careful not to fall in love with him. Unless she wanted her heart smashed to smithereens.

5

Emma walked into the gallery with the thought that she finally understood the expression, "walking on eggshells." For one thing her high-heeled boots thrust her into a balancing act. For another, Keane Moss was famously hot tempered and he was bound to be somewhat wound up from the excitement of the opening even before he discovered she was absconding with one of the artists.

"Keane," Darias called out to him as they entered. The show would open in about fifteen minutes, and caterers were fussing over champagne and miniature pastries. "I believe you've met my fiancée."

Keane shone his brightest social smile on her, then seemed to be searching his brain for something.

"It's me, Emma," she finally said. Did she look so different?

He lifted up his reading glasses. "Good God." He looked at Darias. "Am I missing something?"

"We're announcing our engagement tonight. Rather a whirlwind affair." He shot her a conspiratorial glance. Adrenaline surged through her at the memory that she couldn't tell *anyone* about their plan.

Ever.

"How long have you two known each other?" Keane looked from one to the other, and at the big rock on her finger, blinking.

"Forever," said Darias, before she had time to form a thought. She realized that they probably should have some story made up. "I've been half in love with her all my life."

Apparently Darias didn't have any problem making up nonsense on the fly. Another reason to be wary of him.

Keane tipped his head to one side, and his silver mane flopped sideways. "Now that I know the background, I can see the influence in your latest series."

Now it was her turn to blink. She snuck a glance over her boss's shoulder at the huge triptych of canvases on the wall behind him. A slender female form was dimly visible, emerging from a dark background in the canvas on the far right.

"Absolutely," said Darias.

"Well, you are a dark horse." Keane pocketed his reading glasses. "I wish you'd said something earlier. I'm sure I could have got the *LA Times* to come."

"We prefer to keep things low-key," said Darias, with a warm glance at her that made her heart jump. If she didn't know better, even she might be convinced that he was madly in love with her.

Now Keane fixed his beady stare on her. "I imagine this means I'll be losing you as my desk girl."

She shrugged and tried to look apologetic. "We are moving abroad."

"Of course you are. Well, congratulations, my dear." Her boss leaned in and kissed her on both cheeks as if she were a wealthy patron, rather than a low-paid dogsbody. His cologne assaulted her nostrils, and she tried not to sneeze. "I do hope I'll be invited to the wedding."

Once the guests started to arrive, Keane introduced everyone to the newly engaged couple as if they were his special scoop. Darias threaded his arm through hers, which was both alarming and invigorating.

Emma managed to keep a bright smile on her face and act like she wasn't every bit as surprised as they were by this new turn of events. She really wished they could take a quick break and discuss the story of where and how they met, but Darias didn't seem at all fazed by all the questions so she just let him handle it.

She was merely a paid employee in this situation, after all.

A couple of local tabloids showed up and took pictures. A reporter peppered her with questions, and she told the truth. "Yes, I never dreamed I would marry a prince." And: "I hope I can rise to the challenge of being queen." The whole thing was so surreal that she began to wonder if it was some kind of crazy anxiety dream and she was about to wake up in her own bed.

"We're leaving now, Keane. Early flight

tomorrow." Darias's words sent a shudder of relief through her whole overwrought body.

Keane beamed. "We've sold more than half the show already. I suppose I'll have to forgive you for stealing a valued employee." He kissed her on both cheeks again. His cheeks were soft as a baby's bottom. "See you again soon!"

Emma staggered out, clinging to Darias's arm out of necessity caused by her unaccustomed high heels and a pervasive sense of shock. She didn't dare speak until they were safely inside his SUV. "Did I do okay? I'm not much of an actress."

"You were perfect." A smile stretched his broad mouth. "No one suspected for a moment that I only met you yesterday."

"We really need to get our backstory straight. I think you told one man that we met in France. I've never been to France."

"We'll have to fix that." He looked totally unfazed as he pulled out into the dark street. "But you're right. We need a story that your friends and relatives will believe. What do you suggest?"

She racked her brain. It was hard to come up with ways that one would run across a crowned head of state in New Jersey. "Perhaps we could say that we met in Central Park. Maybe a few years ago, when I was still in college, and that we've kept in touch ever since."

He laughed. "My last two girlfriends might not like that, but it works for me. And we can say we reconnected last Christmas when we met at a party—I was single by then—then fell madly in love."

She nodded. "That works. But why haven't I met

any of your friends?" She pondered a moment. "I didn't want to go out much as I was still grieving the loss of my mom. That part is true. She passed just before Christmas last year."

"I'm very sorry to hear about your mom." The compassion in his voice touched her.

"Me, too. But I'm glad she's not suffering anymore. She'd really appreciate what you're doing for Jonas." She wondered how her brother was getting on at The Fountains. They'd told her not to visit for at least a week.

"I'm glad I could help. It seems we came into each other's lives at just the right time."

She gasped when Darias opened the door to his loft. The battered steel door had left her totally unprepared for the extreme expanse of space it opened into. Aged-wood flooring stretched a good two hundred feet, with only a small island of modernist furniture over to one side. Tall paintings, some of them half finished, stretched along one wall.

"My studio. I like to live surrounded by my work." He bolted the door and set an alarm. "I'll miss this space."

He led her into an enclosed corner where a door opened to reveal a minimalist bedroom with a low bed and a night table that looked like a slice from an ancient tree. "It's late. We should get some sleep. The pilot will be ready for a dawn departure."

There was only one bed. "Uh, should I sleep on the sofa?"

"Sleeping in the same bed will be necessary to

convince people we are man and wife." He shrugged out of his jacket and hung it in the closet. *Omigosh. Is he just going to undress right in front of me?*

"We're not man and wife yet. I barely know you." Her heart pounded. "Can we start a little slow?"

He looked amused. "Of course. Sandro tells me I'm far too matter-of-fact." He indicated the bed. "You sleep here, and I'll take the sofa. We can even sleep in separate rooms at the palace until the wedding. We can tell them you're traditional." His eyes twinkled. "My mother will like that. And after the wedding, of course, I'll be gentle with you." His mouth hitched slightly.

Adrenaline spiked through her. "Be gentle with me? We're not going to—" Her brain raced. "You never said anything about sex."

"It's true." He looked wistful. "I never did." His dark eyes drifted over her face, sparking heat and desire that frightened her.

If she had sex with him, it would be hard to keep her feelings under tight control. There was a reason they called it *making love*. "We're just pretending to be married, so there's no reason for that pretense to continue behind closed doors."

"In olden times the whole family would wait outside the young couple's bedroom for proof that the marriage was consummated and the new bride was still a virgin."

She shivered. "I hope times have changed. Besides, I'm not a virgin."

"Luckily, that's no longer a requirement." He grinned, mischievous. "I guess I'm fortunate you don't have a boyfriend to break up with."

"I don't have time for dating."

"You must have men following you everywhere."

"Not really." She shrugged. "My friend Liz said I come across as an ice queen."

"A queen, certainly." He chuckled. "I can see that men would be intimidated by you."

"Not you, though, apparently."

"No." Laughter danced in his eyes. "Not me. But for tonight I'll take the sofa. My friends from abroad sleep on it all the time so I'm told it's comfortable."

"I appreciate it." She waited for him to leave. Was he just going to stand there? Or maybe strip naked and then stroll out? Heat flashed over her at that last prospect. "Do you need me to leave so you can get what you need?"

"Oh, you want privacy. I'll just brush my teeth."

And grab your pajamas. She hoped he had some. She wasn't ready to see that tall, broad-shouldered physique naked. Not just yet. She needed some time to prepare herself for that—and all the other strange new experiences coming her way.

"The sheets are clean. The maid came this morning."

"Great. Thanks." She should be relieved that the sheets wouldn't bear his intoxicating man scent. She wasn't ready to spend the night with that either.

He finally left and closed the door behind him, and she changed into her sleep shirt as fast as she could in case he came back for something. His bed was insanely comfortable, a huge change from her lumpy secondhand mattress she'd put out by the curb today. She hadn't even told her landlady she was moving yet.

She didn't sleep a wink last night and now she was so overtired she could barely see straight, but her brain wouldn't settle down.

She drew in a deep breath. Jonas was safely at The Fountains, she was heading out on an adventure, and she'd just have to take this journey one step at a time.

"It's time to get ready." Darias's deep voice roused her from a deathlike sleep. It took her a few moments to figure out who he was and where she was.

"I'll be ready in a moment." She needed a shower to wake her up, and after checking that the bathroom door locked, she took one with water so hot it made her skin red. She dressed in a designer casual outfit of gray jeans and a soft, patterned shirt, with some cute ankle boots. It was easy to look good with this kind of expensive wardrobe.

Darias looked at her with approval when she stepped out of the bedroom. "As we fly I'll tell you more about my family." They'd gotten sidetracked last time he'd started.

She nodded. "I've met your brother Sandro, and you mentioned your twin, Beatriz."

His steady brown gaze unnerved her slightly. "I have other brothers and sisters. There are seven more of them."

"Seven?" She stared, panic flaring through her. How could she remember that many names?

He simply smiled. "Let's go."

6

During the flight, Darias filled her in on all his siblings' unusual names and told her a little about them.

Each one sounded more intimidating than the last. She didn't want to hear any more about how Rigo graduated from Harvard Law School and that little Lina, the baby of the family, was studying philosophy at Oxford. "Won't they see right through me? They sound like geniuses."

He laughed. "The smarter people are, the easier it is to fool them."

"Is that a fact?"

"More of an observation. It has to do with confidence."

"Then you must be easy to fool."

"Quite possibly, but only once."

She laughed, and grew bold. "Have you been in love before?" It wasn't such a strange question.

He shook his head. A wry expression haunted his eyes. "I used to dream of it but sooner or later they all turn out to be more interested in my title or my money than the real me."

"Is that why you decided to marry someone who just wants your money?" The situation was laughable.

"Why not? It's all cut and dried and no one's faking anything. Maybe one day I'll fall in love but it's not the kind of thing you can rush and I'm under a deadline here." A smile tugged at the corner of his mouth.

He was already looking ahead to love affairs after this weird business arrangement came to an end. Why did that make her heart sink?

"What kind of woman do you think you could love?" She was curious.

He frowned slightly, pondering her question— which warmed her heart when he could easily have blown it off with a glib answer. "Someone like my mom." He lifted a brow. "She's warm, funny, intelligent, caring and beautiful."

"I bet she'd be touched to hear you say that." Emma was also touched. They always said that how a guy treated his mom was a vision in to the future of his romantic relationships. "I can't wait to meet her."

"She's wonderful. She always encouraged me to pursue art, even when others thought it a foolish waste of time."

"Art is your passion."

He nodded slowly. "Always has been."

"Maybe no woman can compete?"

"You might be right."

Good to know. Darias had thoroughly warned her off falling in love with him and she'd just have to keep that in mind during all those long dark nights in his presence.

He tilted his head and peered at her. "What about you? Have you ever been in love?"

"Not even close. I'm too busy."

"You can't have been too busy for your whole life."

She sighed. "Between school, part time jobs, my crazy brother and trying to help my mom keep things together, I didn't have time for fun."

"What was your mom like?"

She inhaled as sadness welled inside her. "Very sweet, funny, loving. Totally impractical. She lived in a sort of dreamworld. She wore an engagement ring my dad had given her once—they never did get married—even after he died. She was a true romantic even when there was nothing whatsoever to be romantic about."

"I'm sorry to hear about your dad."

"It's okay. He died when I was young—a heroin overdose. I barely even remember him."

"I'm surprised that didn't scare your brother off drugs."

"You'd think it would but I suppose he has the same head-in-the-clouds approach to life as the rest of my family. I don't know why I turned out to be the steady, boring one." She laughed, but it was rather forced. "I've prided myself on being dull and staying out of trouble."

"I don't think you're dull at all. I think you're very adventurous to agree to my madcap scheme and I promise you it will be worth your while."

"Even if I can't right the tell-all biography about it," she teased.

"What kind of man do you think would be right for you?" His eyes sparkled with curiosity.

Tall, dark, handsome, kind, intelligent, rakish, artistic, royal—she wanted to tease him again but didn't dare. He really was too delicious. And totally unsuitable. "Someone dull, I suppose. Maybe another teacher. Or a school administrator."

He chuckled. "You can't pick your future love by their career. You have to go on personality, compatibility, chemistry."

"Even if he's an undertaker?"

"Especially then." They both laughed and their conversation flowed on in the same easy manner, despite the long trip.

Once they'd crossed the Atlantic, Darias pointed out the Pyrenees as they flew over Spain and France, and she felt her anticipation—and terror—growing as he announced they were now flying over Switzerland and the Alps of Northern Italy, drawing closer to the high peaks.

"My homeland," he announced with a flourish, as a forbidding range of snowcapped mountains subsided into lush green fields dotted with tiny cows. "I always feel something when I fly back here."

"I guess that's lucky, given your situation."

"Truth."

A limo picked them up at the airport. As they pulled onto the road, a terrifying thought seized her. "Have you told your mom that..." She blinked. "That we..."

"That we're getting married? No."

"Why?" She felt her eyes grow wide. "Wouldn't it be easier to break the news before she meets me?"

He shook his head, confident as ever. "If I told her over the phone, she'd be full of hard-to-answer questions. When she's standing talking to you, they'll fly out of her mind and she'll be filled with joy."

"There's that dangerous confidence again." She glanced at the back of the driver's head. Of course she was only voicing worries that any nervous new fiancée might think. "What if she hates me?"

"She couldn't hate anyone. She's the most loving soul in the world."

Emma certainly couldn't question that in front of the driver. "I look forward to meeting her," she lied. "What should I call her?"

"Call her mama."

Emma's nerves ratcheted tighter as they drove into a pretty town with a mix of medieval and eighteenth-century buildings. Even the streets were picturesque, with smooth cobbles and larger stones laid in two tracks for carriage wheels.

"This is Casteleone, the town that grew up around my ancestors' old castle. We're headed to a newer palace where my mom and dad lived."

"It's incredibly beautiful."

"Casteleone has a long tradition of artists, architects and craftsmen." He looked out the window. "I'm proud to follow in their footsteps."

They drove through a tall set of black iron gates with elaborate crests tooled into the railings. Behind them rose a baroque palace, three stories tall, with impressive arched windows and long balconies.

Mama. This was not going to be easy!

"Relax. You'll be fine."

"Am I breathing heavy or something?" She was trying her hardest to appear nonchalant.

"You seem a little tense."

"Wouldn't you be?"

A smile tugged at one corner of his mouth. "Quite possibly."

As the car pulled in front of the main doors, they opened and an elegant blonde woman appeared, flanked by two gray-uniformed staffers. She came down the steps as they opened their doors and climbed out.

"Mama, I missed you." Darias kissed her on both cheeks, then again on the first one. "How are you holding up?"

"I'm trying to do things as Papa would have wanted." She held Darias's face in her hands. "I do miss him."

"I know, Mama." He stroked her hair. They were a very touchy-feely family. Emma's heart ached to remember that her mom had been like that, too. "I have someone for you to meet."

His mom looked over at Emma for the first time, and a curious expression crossed her face. She looked back at Darias, now expectant.

Darias held out his hand for Emma to come join them. Heart pounding, she took cautious steps across the white marble pavers. "Mama, this is Emma Ricci. I've proposed marriage to her, and she's agreed. She will be my wife."

Emma managed a shaky smile. The way he described their union sounded rather businesslike—which it was—and didn't feel as fake as she'd imagined.

"Emma?" His mom focused her full attention on her, now holding out both hands to take one of Emma's. "I'm so thrilled to meet you." Her voice rang with surprise but also pleasure. She turned to her son. "Darias, why have you been keeping this beautiful young lady a secret from me?"

"You know how you are, Mama. You would have peppered me with questions that I wasn't ready to answer."

"And here your aunt and I have spent the last three days racking our brains and making phone calls all over Europe, looking for a bride for you." She tutted, then turned back to Emma. "But I'm thrilled that we no longer need to find one. Welcome to the family, Emma."

Before Emma could draw breath, she was enveloped in a deep hug. Worse yet, she could hear sobs rising in Darias's mom's chest as she was overcome with emotion. Emma tried to hug her back without feeling like too much of a heel. Still, she couldn't come up with one single thing to say except, "Thank you."

"Come in. Come in!" Now alive with excitement, Darias's mom turned to climb the steps. "We must show Emma around."

"She might be tired after our long flight, Mama."

"I'm fine, really," she protested. She wanted to fulfill her role to the best of her ability. "I'd love to see the palace."

"You'll live here with Darias, I hope." His mom squeezed her arm as they reached a vast foyer of white marble. "The kings of Altaleone have lived here since the seventeen hundreds. Darias's grandmother, the late queen, preferred a smaller residence in the center of town, so my husband and I lived here. I'll move to the late queen's house if it pleases Darias."

"You shall live wherever you like, Mama." Darias slid his arm around her waist and kissed her on the forehead. Emma was touched by how much he cared about his mom—enough to create an expensive charade just to keep her happy.

"Have the police made any discoveries?" Darias's question tugged her back to the moment.

"Not a one!" His mom's voice rang with distress. "I don't understand how there can be no clues or evidence after the way they died. It was clearly murder."

"We'll get to the bottom of it. I've wrapped up my business in New York, and I can stay here now and focus on the investigation. This afternoon I want to visit the crime scene again."

"It's under heavy guard right now." His mom sighed. "Do be careful, sweetheart. We still don't know why they did this. As the next in line, you could be in grave danger."

"I'll watch my back. And I have a feeling a number of experienced security guards will be doing the same thing." He shot her a wry smile.

"Yes. Security is greatly increased. We've hired an expert. An ex–foreign legion man with a reputation for solving this kind of crime. He thinks we should bug every room in the palace. He suspects an inside job."

Darias's eyes widened. "I hope he hasn't bugged my chambers. I don't think my new bride and I would enjoy our wedding night much if we thought half the guards in the palace were listening in."

His mother laughed. "Of course not, darling. I told him his idea was nonsense, anyway. We're all family here, and we look out for each other."

Emma released a taut breath she hadn't realized she was holding. It would be truly awkward if there was nowhere private for her to talk to Darias. Though she should be mindful that anywhere could be bugged, even their cars.

Darias introduced her to his twin sister, Beatriz, a solemn brunette beauty who seemed deeply surprised to meet his new fiancée, and who explained that the rest of their siblings had all rushed back to their respective careers and schools, leaving her to take care of their mom alone.

"I'm sorry I had to go back to New York. Poor Keane had been putting that show together for months. I couldn't let him down."

"You do realize that you're going to have to stop painting now, right?" said Beatriz. "You have bigger responsibilities. This trip back to New York so soon after the funeral and right before the coronation was really uncalled for."

"I had to convince my bride to return with me." Darias slid his arm around Emma in a proprietary fashion that made her skin tingle. Beatriz's shapely brows lowered slightly. Emma got the feeling that there was more than a little tension between them. Not surprising since he was about to become King and she wasn't—yet she was the one left there to hold down the fort.

"I suppose it is a relief that you have a bride. Though Mama and Aunt Liesel put together an impressive list of prospects for you. It's almost a shame to see their hard work go to waste. I had no idea that Europe had so many young royals left in it." Beatriz snuck a glance at Emma, who'd never felt less royal in her life.

"Perhaps they'll be a good fit for Rigo or Sandro." Darias leaned in and kissed Emma on the cheek. Heat flashed through her, and even when he pulled back she felt as if his lips had seared an impression on her skin. Her pulse raced, and she realized she was staring.

He's just trying to convince his sister this is real.

Problem was, it felt way too real. Warmth now flooded her body, which probably would have liked to turn his quick kiss into something a lot more meaningful. "Uh," she turned to Beatriz. "Could I use the bathroom?"

Beatriz blinked, as if astonished that such a mundane need should be mentioned in public. "Of course, my dear," offered Darias's mom. "Let me show you where it is. Come with me"

She threaded her arm through Emma's and led her off along a wide hallway with an intricate pattern of black and white marble on the floor.

Out of the frying pan and into the fire!

Emma tried to walk in as dignified a manner as possible, which wasn't easy since her cute ankle boots had a narrow heel and the floor was polished and slick. His mom didn't say anything until they had rounded a corner and entered a second hallway, lined with tall wood doors surrounded by frothy white carvings, in a sea of light blue wall. How far away was this bathroom, anyway?

"I can't understand why Darias never mentioned you to me," she said at last. "The subject of his marriage came up several times at the funeral, and he never said a thing." Emma didn't dare look at her. She was afraid of the suspicious expression she'd see. "I suppose he wanted to ask you in person first." She took Emma's hand and squeezed it. "That's so romantic, really. I'm rather surprised."

So Darias's mother didn't think him romantic? She was right. He'd hired her to avoid the tiresome prospect of a real romance. "I was surprised myself. But I'm very happy," she stammered.

All true, really. Her brother was finally safe from junkies and mobsters and had a chance to get back on his feet. She'd have an adventure and head home to a nice nest egg.

"So are we all, Emma. You have no idea! His aunt and I were so worried he wouldn't agree to marry anyone, and there's an ancient edict that the king must be married to take the throne. Such requirements were rather common in the old days; I suppose to ensure that the royal line continues with at least one legitimate heir. I wanted his father to abolish it, but I'm afraid he rather approved of it."

Emma watched with horror as tears filled the older woman's eyes. "Do excuse me. I'm not quite used to the idea that he's gone."

"I'm so sorry for your loss." Emma wanted to reach out and soothe her, but that might be against royal etiquette and she didn't want to commit any gaffes. Darias's mom pushed open a tall door and led her into a wide chamber with an elaborate parquet wood floor and some elegantly upholstered blue-and-ivory chairs. Huge portraits of eighteenth-century ancestors peered down at her as she picked her way across the ornate woodwork.

Where was this toilet? In Switzerland?

"It's not far now." Darias's mom turned to her with a smile. Emma immediately panicked that she had the ability to read minds. "This palace was built back when everyone used chamber pots, and this first floor is all formal galleries that didn't really lend themselves to having bathrooms installed. Don't worry, all the bedrooms have an en suite these days."

"That is a relief. I don't fancy making a trek like this in the middle of the night."

They both laughed, and it was a relief to have some kind of normal conversation with her future mother-in-law, even if she'd only know her for one year.

Finally, his mom gestured to a smaller, white-painted door in the corner of a striking blue-and-yellow room with a grand piano in one corner. "They put a lavatory in here because it was the old men's smoking room. They needed somewhere to stagger to after they'd been hitting the champagne too hard. Darias's grandmother always hated the room and had it redecorated as feminine as possible when she took over." His mom's conspiratorial smile made her smile back with genuine warmth. "Do you think you can find your way back to us?"

"Sure." Emma tried not to look panicked. If she could make her way back to the group without GPS, it would be a miracle. When she emerged, she could barely remember if she should turn left or right. The room next door had sage green furnishings. That way.

A pretty staffer in a gray uniform smiled at her and she smiled back, hoping that wasn't a breach of decorum. Her heels made a fearful noise as she headed into the marble corridor. Doors stretched in either direction for what seemed like miles. Could she hear voices?

She heard two people nearby, murmuring in what sounded like French, but they hushed as she came closer and she never saw them.

"Emma." Darias's voice filled her with relief. "We're back this way."

"I got confused."

"You'll get the hang of it. My mom loves you already."

"She's very sweet, just like you said."

"See? Everything will work out fine."

She glanced around, wondering if anyone could read into his words. She wanted to warn him that they weren't alone. "I just heard two people speaking French nearby."

"Probably staff." He didn't look worried. "Altaleone is situated in a place where several cultures meet. You'll hear people speaking Italian, German, French and, of course, English. That's what we grew up speaking. The Altaleone language is an obscure dialect of Italian that isn't very useful outside of our borders. We'll head to your room to unpack."

"*My* room?"

"Until the wedding." He lifted a brow slightly. "I told my mom you were superstitious and wanted us to sleep apart until then."

"Thank you." She glanced around. Not that she'd said anything at all incriminating. It was going to take her a while to relax into this charade.

The palace seemed to shrink to manageable size as she kept pace with Darias back to the foyer, then headed up a grand, winding staircase to the second floor. Tall portraits lined the walls of the staircase.

"Are these your ancestors?"

"Yes. That one is Ludovico Leone, who built this palace." He pointed to a tall man in a powdered wig and a long velvet coat, with two black dogs at his heels. "Legend in the village says that he imprisoned his enemies in the wine cellar until they starved, then fed them to his dogs."

"What?" She shivered, almost afraid to look at the confident, pink-cheeked man in the painting. "Is that true?"

"There's no way to know for sure, but I suspect it was a PR campaign to keep his creditors at arm's length. This was a very expensive palace to build." She laughed. "I'd imagine. Not a bad strategy, either."

"The Altaleone people are known for being wily and defensive. That's the main reason our tiny nation is still here despite all the upheaval over the last centuries."

"That and the forbidding mountains all around you."

"Those too." He put his hand on a shiny brass door handle and turned it. The door opened to reveal a large, well-lit room with a huge four-poster bed covered in blue velvet brocade.

"I'll certainly feel like a princess sleeping in here."

She jumped when the door opened behind her. A young man in a gray uniform carried her two bags.

"He'll unpack for you," said Darias.

"Oh, no. I'd much rather do it myself." She had packed a copy of their contract, which, now that she thought about it, was a very stupid idea. Not being used to living in a palace, she hadn't considered the total lack of privacy. She'd have to find a way to burn that as soon as possible.

"I'll leave you to it. Lunch will be downstairs in about forty-five minutes. Be warned. My mom and Beatriz are already planning your wedding."

"My wedding? It's your wedding, too."

"Oh, yes." He looked almost surprised. "So it is."

7

Emma unpacked her bags, hiding the contract inside the folder with her birth certificate, passport and other important papers.

Then she pulled it out. If someone was to snoop through her things, looking for damning information about her, surely that would be the first place they'd look. After glancing around the room, she reached up and stuck the three typed pages up on top of the scrolled wardrobe, where they were hidden behind a decorative flourish on the front.

She dusted off her hands, then changed for lunch into a pair of dark brown pants and a fitted blouse. Everyone was quite smart—almost business casual—so she figured this would fit in. She combed her hair and put on some lipstick, then took a deep breath and headed downstairs.

She followed the sound of voices to a bright dining room with a shiny wood table set for a meal.

"Emma, come join us quick, before Darias gets here." His mom was beaming. "I think a woman should choose the decorations for her own wedding, and he's such an artiste he'll probably have strong ideas about it."

Emma doubted that, since he didn't consider this to be a real wedding at all. "I'm open to anything you suggest," she said, sitting in the chair his mom indicated. Beatriz sat opposite her, and the table was covered with glossy pages imprinted with the logo of some expensive design firm. "It looks like you've made progress already."

To her surprise Darias's mom seemed to blush slightly, her neck reddening. "I'm sure it sounds terrible, but I've been thinking about it all week. It was the only way I could get my mind off the awful events and the sadness of the funeral. We've been looking at monogrammed glasses and flower arrangements and the most beautiful cakes, even though we didn't know who Darias would marry. I thought we were going to have to truck in a bride along with the extra chairs and napkins. I'm just so very happy that he brought you here."

Emma blinked. "Me, too." Darias really was doing his mom a favor by contracting his own bride. Otherwise his mom and sister would have probably arranged his marriage using a glossy stack of pictures of European nobility similar to these pages of expensive wedding ornaments.

"What style of dress did you have in mind?" Beatriz asked.

Emma paused. She had never given a single moment's thought to a wedding, let alone a dress for one. And she had no idea what would be considered appropriate for a royal bride. "I'm not sure, but I'm guessing it should be long and white?"

"I think we should have the local dressmaker

come and bring some samples. She's quite famous for her wedding dresses. And we can choose the bridesmaid dresses, too. Will you be flying many friends out?"

Emma froze. She hadn't even told her friends about Darias. She'd been so caught up in her mom's illness and her two jobs that she'd lost touch with most of them lately. "I wasn't planning to."

"Your parents will be coming, though?" Darias's mom looked hopeful but wary.

"I'm afraid they've both passed."

"Oh, goodness." Her smooth brow furrowed. "You're all alone?"

"I have a brother, but he's…busy." She probably wouldn't be thrilled to hear that her beloved firstborn son was marrying someone with a junkie in the family, let alone that he was paying for the junkie's rehab. "He won't be able to come either." Oh, dear. This wasn't going well.

Darias's mom's faced softened, and Emma startled when she almost looked like her eyes were going to fill with tears. "Then, my dear, you have absolutely come to the right place, and we welcome you all the more warmly into our family." She took Emma's hand and squeezed it. Emma felt sudden tears rise unexpectedly at the warm gesture. "Darias's sisters can be your bridesmaids. They'll be thrilled to play a part in the wedding."

Emma snuck a glance at Beatriz, who didn't look entirely enraptured by the idea but stiffly said, "Of course we would."

"I know it's very soon to suggest this, but…."

Darias's mom hesitated. "Would you consider calling me mama? I would never presume to take the place of your own dear mother, but I do hope you'll count on me for anything you need."

Uh-oh. Hot tears rolled down Emma's cheeks. "That's so very kind of you." And of course Darias was right again. "I'd be very pleased to." As long as she could handle each sharp stab of guilt she felt at knowing this was a business arrangement, not a true family bond being created. She wiped awkwardly at her eyes with the back of her hands. "I'm sorry. I'm a bit overwhelmed."

"Of course you are," said Darias's mom softly. She pulled a perfectly pressed white monogrammed handkerchief from her pocket and handed it to Emma. "A new country, a wedding, a new life—it's enough to overwhelm anyone. Beatriz and I will do our best to make you feel at home."

"Of course," said Beatriz unconvincingly. "I'll call the dressmaker."

Darias climbed in his car, determined to drive out to the old palace, where his father and grandfather had been murdered, before one more person could try to stop him. He'd made it out there once during the frantic funeral preparations, but the site had still been a police crime scene and he couldn't seem to get any straight answers from anyone, even about how the bodies had been found.

Newspaper accounts were disturbingly vague, and his mom wouldn't tell him anything other than to warn him to "be careful." Two members of the royal family dead in one day and not one suspect arrested? The injustice made his blood boil.

He left the narrow, cobbled streets of Casteleone behind and headed out into the sheep meadows outside the town. The dirt road wound up toward hillsides covered with flowers in the warm summer sunshine. The old palace was in a remote location and had once been the summer playground of his ancestors but was now rarely visited. He had never even been there himself until a week ago.

Darias drummed his fingers on the steering wheel as he drove. He hoped Emma was getting along okay with his mother and sister. So far she seemed like she would work out just fine. Except that he was far more attracted to her than he cared to admit.

Still, if a man couldn't keep his hands off a woman in a business situation—which this was— he was hardly a man at all. He would simply have to keep reminding himself that he was doing this for the good of Altaleone and his family.

A herd of red-and-white cows did not look up from their grazing as he drove past. He shifted gears as the road grew steeper, winding toward the mountains. The dry dirt road bore the tracks of many cars, not simply the tractors that would normally pass this way. Police, detectives, the so-called security experts that the family had hired, any of these people might be milling around when he arrived at the old palace. He resolved to treat them all with suspicion.

And, if his mother was correct, he'd do well to be

wary of them. They still had no idea why the royal family had been targeted.

The cows gave way to a herd of goats wandering across the fields with bells around their necks, much as they must have done for hundreds of years. Time stood still in Altaleone—it was one of the things he liked least about the place. But now that the serenity of his homeland had been disturbed, he took the affront very personally. He intended to find the killers and restore peace to his family and his nation.

There were only two cars in the wide courtyard in front of the palace. One, a police vehicle, parked almost directly in front of the main door, as if barricading it. Darias's hackles rose. This house was Leone family property. He parked further away, by the second car, a black SUV with Altaleone plates.

"Hello?" His voice echoed off the stone facade. He had no desire to surprise the security and get shot. "Who's there?"

He climbed the smooth stone steps toward the door, which stood ajar. Again, his sense of family honor felt offended by the casual treatment of this ancient family home. Even if no one had lived there for decades.

Darias braced himself as he stepped into the cool gloom of the interior. This remote building always gave him the chills. And where was everyone?

"Darias Leone here," he said, in as authoritative a tone as he could muster.

A figure dressed in black stepped out of the shadows to his left. Adrenaline coursed through Darias's body, but he simply lifted his chin as a tall man walked toward him.

"Gibran Al Nazariyah. Your family has retained me to investigate the murders and secure your safety.

Gibran didn't hold out his hand, but Darias wanted to feel his handshake and see what he was made of, so he held out his. Firm, solid, reasonably trustworthy. "Now that I'm back here for good, I want answers and I won't leave until I get some. The details I've heard are far too vague. Where exactly was my grandmother—the queen—found?

Gibran's poker face barely moved. "The circumstances were unusual."

"I imagine that could be said for most murders. Tell me the exact details. I know it was in an upstairs room." He hadn't even been permitted entry when he'd returned for the funeral. "Take me there."

Gibran led the way up a dusty staircase of inlaid red and white stone. The family portraits on the walls had been removed, leaving ghostly outlines. As they reached the top of the stairs, Darias saw a police guard standing outside a tall doorway.

"Why is he here?"

"We don't want to give anyone the opportunity to tamper with the evidence." Darias walked past the guard into the room. He was about to ask what evidence, but the words withered on his lips. In the center of the room was a tall wooden device with a hole in the middle like a medieval stocks where someone's head would poke through. On the floor nearby, surrounded by strips of yellow police tape, lay a black leather flogger of the type used in BDSM play.

Darias stared. A horrible feeling clawed at the inside of his gut. "Was she…?" He couldn't bring himself to ask the question.

Gibran spoke. "She was found fastened inside the stocks. Dressed in a one-piece black leather suit."

Darias drew in a deep breath to steady himself. "How was she killed?"

"Asphyxiation." Gibran's voice was low, professional. Darias could barely bring himself to look the other man in the eye, even though Gibran had probably not seen his grandmother in this compromising situation. He had been hired after the events transpired. "When I first arrived, I entertained the scenario that the situation was consensual. But of course her son being found murdered in a room nearby made that unlikely."

"My grandmother would most certainly never have participated in bondage-style activities," said Darias grimly. "She was a very proper lady. A queen in every sense of the word."

Gibran stared at the empty stocks for a moment. "Often it is people in positions of power who most feel the need for this kind of release."

"Never." He hoped he would be able to banish the vision of his elegant and charming grandmother dressed in black leather from his mind. The idea appalled him. "Someone has arranged this disgusting scene to smear my family's reputation."

Gibran's eyes narrowed slightly. "Were you aware that she and your father were both members of a secret society called the Cross of Blood?"

Darias paused, trying to gather his thoughts. "I

was aware. However, the Cross of Blood is an ancient society dating back to the Crusades. They have meetings of some sort, perhaps once a year. At one point my father tried to convince me to join. I thought it would be boring so I refused. I hardly think he would have invited me to join some kinky sex club." Just talking about his beloved and respected family members in this manner made his blood boil and his fingers curl into fists. "We need to find out who did this."

Gibran cleared his throat. "Our investigation is being hampered by your mother's insistence that we keep the circumstances surrounding the deaths completely secret."

Darias took another look at the stocks. "I agree with her. At least until we have some idea what was going on, we should keep completely quiet about this. I couldn't bear for my grandmother's reputation to be tarnished by someone's idea of a cruel joke."

"I understand."

"And my father—" Darias was almost afraid to ask. And very little scared him. "What were the circumstances of his death?"

Gibran rubbed a hand over his mouth. "You are aware that he was stabbed with a sword?"

"Yes, I had heard that much. However, I suspect there is more to the story."

"Come with me." Gibran exited the room with a nod to the police guard. He turned right and headed further along the hallway to where another door was closed with yellow police tape. "His body was found in here." He pulled back the tape and opened the door. "I'm afraid the scene is very bloody. On my instructions, they've left the room exactly as it was found."

Darias peered past him into the gloomy interior of what must once have been a large bedroom, now devoid of furniture. As he made out the dark shadows on the floor and realized that they were blood—his father's blood—his stomach churned and he fought a powerful urge to vomit.

He steeled himself to face the horrifying scene and walked into the room. "Tell me the exact circumstances. Don't hold anything back."

Gibran cleared his throat. "He was found facedown in the center of the room. Naked."

Darias closed his eyes and inhaled, trying to ground himself. "And the weapon?"

"Was still sticking out of his back when he was found."

"Did it have fingerprints on it?"

"Many." Gibran grimaced. "Too many. Nothing we could work with. We suspect the murderer wore gloves and that the fingerprints we found were older. The weapon was a family heirloom usually kept in the royal armory."

"Who removed it?"

"No one knows. It may have been missing for some time."

"What? The royal armory is where the crown jewels are kept. There is a single diamond in there worth twenty-three million dollars. How can items just vanish?"

"We're looking into it."

Darias blew out hard, frustration growing to boiling point. "The bodies were found by police sent out to look for the missing persons. Who sounded the alarm?"

Gibran hesitated again, his eyes narrowing in that disconcerting fashion. "That's the official story but the truth is that the bodies were found by your mother. She came out here to look for your father."

"What made her think he'd be here?"

"She said he came to meetings here with a private club that he belonged to."

"Good lord. So she saw——" He stared down at the shadows of dried blood on the floor.

"I'm afraid she saw it all. We are under instructions to keep that secret, too."

Darias blinked. How could his mother be thumbing through wedding brochures after witnessing such horrifying scenes? He shook his head. It didn't bear thinking about.

"She's a suspect, of course."

"What?" Darias's voice boomed off the walls. "Never. Impossible."

"A murderer is often the first person found at the scene of a crime, for obvious reasons. Of course it's awkward for the police to even try to question a member of the royal family. So they didn't."

"I should hope not." Darias frowned, assaulted by these fresh horrors that his mother had endured. He shouldn't have gone back to New York after the funeral. Not for just another gallery show— but he'd had no idea.

Why didn't she tell him? "I'll talk to her myself, but I'm sure she had nothing to do with this." His skin crawled at the sight of all the blood, etched in dried waves on the floor. "There was nothing else in the room?"

"Nothing. His clothes were folded up in the corner of a room downstairs."

"So he walked up here naked?" Darias couldn't believe that for a minute.

"We have no way to know for sure."

"Footprints, on the stone tiles?"

Gibran shrugged. "The early investigations obliterated all footprints outside the immediate crime scenes. The local law enforcement was not well prepared for such a crime."

"I wouldn't expect them to be. We haven't had a murder in Altaleone in years." He shook his head. "Do you have any theories on motive?"

Gibran tilted his head very slightly. "The current ruler and the successor both die in the same night. The person who stands to benefit most is, of course, the next in line."

"Me?" The word exploded out. "First, you all but accuse my mother, and now you're pointing the finger at me? I wasn't even on the continent of Europe when the murders happened. I was in New York. I suppose you suspect that my mother and I formed a conspiracy—" His voice boomed through the empty halls. "I should fire you for even suggesting it."

"You certainly can." This man was totally unruffled. "But I have a strong track record of solving similar crimes. A complex crime like this, where motive and even method are obfuscated, takes time and cunning to solve. As much time and cunning as the crime took to plan and execute."

Darias turned and walked from the room and down the stairs. He could hear Gibran striding behind him. "Find the killers. And I want to be informed immediately about every step of the investigation. You can continue to keep the ugly details hidden from the press but not from me, do you understand?"

"Of course. And I would prefer if you were under constant guard. If you are not the murderer—" Gibran's eyes shone with dark mirth. "You must presume that you are in immediate danger."

"I can take care of myself."

Dirt flew as Darias drove back through the remote mountain meadows and descended the gentle hillsides toward the village of Casteleone. Even the royal armory had been violated. And those horrible images were etched into his gentle mother's mind.

He intended to find the killer and make him pay.

But first he had to make sure his queen didn't decide to skip town before the wedding.

8

Emma was drinking mint tea and mostly listening to Beatriz read out an insanely long list of potential wedding guests when Darias burst into the drawing room like a gust of wind.

"You didn't tell me." He stared at his mother like he'd seen a ghost.

She paled. "I couldn't. I couldn't bear it. I still can't...." She rose to her feet.

"Oh, Mama." He strode to her and folded her in his arms, hugging her so close that she almost disappeared into him. Emma's heart squeezed at the sight of so much affection. "I'll find justice for them—for you—I swear it."

"What are you talking about, Darias?" Beatriz put down her pen. "Is there something I should know?"

His mother shook her head quickly.

"There is, isn't there? What happened? Is it about Papa's death?" She rose to her feet, scraping her chair back. "Don't treat me like a child. I was born on the same day as Darias, remember? What the heck is going on?"

Darias's mom glanced at Emma. "We have a new family member with us, my love." Her voice was choked, almost cracking.

Emma rose to her feet now, too. "Uh, I'm just heading up to my bedroom for a moment." Clearly something very heavy was going on—likely to do with the murders—and they needed some privacy. She could make herself scarce.

"Wait," called Darias. "I'm coming with you."

What? She was leaving to give him time alone with his mom. "Okay." She climbed the stairs to her room, listening to Darias's footfalls behind her. She waited until they were somewhat out of earshot. "Did you learn anything new?"

"Did I ever." His face clouded with emotion. "The circumstances of their deaths were calculated to create rumor and scandal. My mother is right to keep them secret." He glanced both ways down the hallway. "I don't know who's listening to us. Come in." He led her into her own bedroom, then to her surprise headed straight for a huge carved wardrobe, opened the door, and climbed in next to her hanging items.

"Are we going to Narnia?"

"Come in." He looked deadly serious.

"Into the wardrobe?"

He looked at her like she might be mildly demented. Then she climbed in with him. It was hard to enter without rubbing against him, and his tempting masculine scent already filled the small space. He closed the door, leaving them in total darkness.

"I can't have anyone overhear us. Even the staff."

Her skin prickled at the tension in his voice. "You suspect someone?"

"I suspect everyone." She cursed the way his low

voice sent a flicker of arousal to her core. "And I don't want anyone to know the details if they don't have to. If only the killer or killers know the circumstances of the deaths, maybe they will reveal themselves by trying to boast about it or stir up scandal."

"I guess I shouldn't ask, then."

"I know you're not involved. You were a total random stranger that I pulled off the streets. You are a disinterested observer here, and I value your opinion."

She listened, intrigued. She was just a paid employee, like the rest of the staff, really. She wasn't sure how she could help.

"They were both found in compromising positions—undressed and in a strange costume—that they must have been coerced into, either verbally or otherwise. My grandmother was arranged as if participating in a kinky sex act. Our security advisor thinks it has to do with an ancient society they belonged to."

"You think it was some kind of ritual that went wrong?"

He hesitated, and she could almost feel his pain and confusion in the air, along with the heat from his body in the tight space. "I just don't know. I realize now that there's a lot I don't know. I'll need to investigate."

"I'd like to help in any way I can."

"I appreciate that. The most important thing is for you to stay safe. For me to protect my mother and my younger siblings. To preserve my own life so I can do my duty to my country. I suppose I should apologize for bringing you into a situation rife with danger and uncertainty, but I swear to keep you safe until you can return home."

"I doubt anyone's interested in me."

"I think *everyone* is interested in you." He paused and, although it was too dark to see, she could imagine a slow smile crossing his mouth. "Everyone in Altaleone and across the world. An unknown young beauty on the arm of one of Europe's most eligible monarchs. It's impossible for them not to be fascinated."

She frowned. Obviously, he was going somewhere with this line of thought. "How does that affect the current situation?"

"Whoever is responsible for the death of my father and grandmother will be burning with curiosity, too. Clearly, they have some kind of plan and you are not a part of it—you can't be—so they will want to know how you affect whatever situation they're trying to bring about. So watch everyone. Pay attention when someone is interested in you. Guard your answers—and tell me *everything*."

"I'll try."

"We'll be together as much as possible, of course, as is natural for a new husband and wife. That will also make it easier for me to shield you from danger."

The way he said the word *danger* sent a frisson of…something—she wasn't sure if it was fear or arousal—shivering through her. Darias did seem like the kind of guy you could count on during a zombie apocalypse. His confidence, strength and sheer size were reassuring. But against an invisible foe with unknown motives? She shivered slightly, even in the close atmosphere of the closet. "I'm sure I'll be fine." She said it to reassure herself as much as him.

"I guarantee it—with my life." His face had moved closer to hers, and she could feel his warm breath on her cheek. Her skin heated. She shifted, bumping awkwardly against the back of the closet and then worse, against him, her arm making contact with his hard chest.

She gasped. "I'm sorry." Touching him felt wrong. Way wrong.

But she wanted to, and the desire was building with every second they stayed inside the tight, warm space of this closet. She had to get out of there—now!

"I can't breathe in here."

He opened the door. Light flooded in, making her blink. He stepped out, then pressed a finger softly to his lips. She nodded, stepping down onto the floor.

Phew! She'd survived that without wrapping her arms around him and planting a wet one on his mouth, but it had been touch and go toward the end. She would definitely have to avoid situations where they were in such close quarters together.

Of course he felt nothing. The attraction was all on her side. That was a relief, of course. Nothing could come of it.

"You should go down and talk to your mom and sister." She inhaled, trying to get her thoughts back on some kind of sensible track. Which wasn't easy now that she could see Darias in all his broad-shouldered, dark-eyed glory. "You should probably tell your sister all the details."

He winced. "I hate to do that."

"She'll feel slighted or left out if you don't." She could tell his sister was upset about being kept in the dark. She would be, too, in her place. Why did she have any less right to know the facts than Darias? "It was her father and grandmother, too."

"I want to protect her from the ugliness. I wish with all my heart that I could have been there to find them instead of my mother."

"Just because they're women doesn't mean they're weak and fragile." She straightened her back a little, not much liking what seemed like a patronizing attitude.

He frowned and studied her for a moment. "My father raised me to protect the family. He talked about it more than once when we were alone."

"You think he had any idea what was coming?"

He shook his head slowly. "But you're right. They are adults the same as I am. We must face the situation and make plans together." His eyes grazed her face for a moment, and she saw something surprising there—respect?—which caused a rumble of strange emotion deep inside her. "I'll see you downstairs for dinner at eight."

Once the door closed behind him she collapsed on the bed. Not only had she fought off an overwhelming urge to kiss Darias on the mouth, she'd now given him a feminist lecture about treating his mother and sister as equals. What next?

Dinner took place in a very grand dining room, under the haughty stare of several velvet- and satin-clad ancestors, but was relatively painless.

They all dressed informally, and discussion centered mostly around the wedding plans, which were already proceeding at warp speed. Emma's dress fitting was arranged for the following day, and his mom and Beatriz argued over the date for the wedding.

"As soon as possible, of course!" said his mother. "Why wait?"

Emma swallowed and forked another bite of the strange casserole into her mouth. The food was delicious, just unfamiliar, along with the shiny silverware that was probably real silver and the two different glasses of no-doubt fabulously expensive wine in front of her.

It was in her interest—and presumably Darias's— to get married as fast as possible, because they had to stay married for one full year in order to meet the rules of the ancient law.

"Your brother wants to marry his beloved as fast as he can, of course." His mom smiled. "Your father was just the same. We only met twice before the wedding, and he told me that he fell in love with me the moment he laid eyes on me." Her smile faded. "It's just so hard to believe that he's gone. I'm sorry. Let's focus on the present. I'm so happy for Darias and Emma. Thank goodness we have something joyous to focus on."

"I just think the people should have a chance to get to know Darias's bride," said Beatriz, eyeing Emma with some suspicion "Until yesterday no one had even heard of her." She turned her gaze to Darias. "Why did you keep Emma such a secret until now?"

"I preferred to keep my private life private. Now

that I will be king, my decisions are of necessity a matter of public interest, but did the people of Altaleone really need to know my every movement before now?"

"Your brother is right, my dear. There's no reason to risk scandal and upset by dating in public."

Beatriz stiffened. "I never do."

"I know, my love, I wasn't accusing you of anything." Her mom frowned. "You're exemplary in every way, and I don't know what any of us would do without you."

Emma looked from Beatriz to Darias. Obviously, there was some longstanding tension here. She had a feeling she might have to watch her back around Beatriz. It was a shame they couldn't just tell her the whole thing was fake. She'd probably be relieved.

But Emma was sworn to secrecy.

"I want the wedding to take place as soon as humanly possible."

"But people must make travel plans," protested Beatriz. "You can't just expect heads of state to clear their calendars at a moment's notice and rush to Altaleone."

"Then we will miss them." Darias smiled at Emma and reached his hand out affectionately to her across the gleaming oak table. She had to think fast for a moment—act like you're really in love!—so she reached out and he grasped her fingers.

Heat rushed through her, unfortunately, at the touch of his skin to hers. She didn't need to act the sudden rush of color and emotion. Hopefully, Darias would just think she was an amazing actress. She really didn't want him to know about these strange new sensations going on inside her.

"Emma and I want to be married next week. We are quite happy to have only the villagers of Casteleone in attendance."

"But what about the family?" Beatriz looked shocked. "Our brothers and sisters have important jobs, school exams. Surely you don't—"

"Somehow I think they'll all manage to make it." Darias squeezed Emma's hand. "And if they don't?" He shrugged. "Their loss."

"I don't know." Beatriz frowned and sipped her wine. "I think it seems too fast. Weirdly fast."

"I think it's wonderful," said his mom, her complexion glowing again. "The people of Altaleone will be so happy to have something to celebrate in the wake of tragedy."

"We'll set the wedding for next Saturday," said Darias, still holding Emma's hand, which was starting to sweat. "It will be a national holiday, which we'll announce tomorrow. Everyone in Altaleone is invited to attend, and we'll have a big buffet feast in the village square."

His mom clapped her hands in delight. "I love it!"

"Can they sew the dress in time?" Beatriz stared.

"Emma will look gorgeous in any dress they have in the store. She can pick one out, and all they have to do is alter it."

"Absolutely," insisted Emma when Darias's mom and Beatriz turned their gazes to her. "I'm sure they'll have something lovely. You must both come with me to help me choose."

"We'd love that, wouldn't we, Beatriz?" Darias's

mom beamed.

"Of course," said Beatriz flatly.

Darias extricated his hand from Emma's, which was now trembling slightly. Darias was in a really big rush to get married. Maybe he thought she might get scared and run off if he waited too long. Maybe he was right.

Emma's first night alone in her grand palace bedroom was tense. The long blue brocade curtains cast weird shadows over the bed, which made her wonder if the building was haunted. It had to be hundreds of years old. Who knew how many people could have died there?

And why had Darias's father and grandmother been murdered? Who would want them dead, and would they be a danger to Darias or other members of the family? Every rustle of expensive fabric and creak in the ancient walls set her nerves on edge.

And she half expected Darias to wander in, features illuminated by moonlight, and claim her.

Maybe because that was what happened in the one ragged dream she managed in an almost sleepless night.

She really shouldn't have taken this job.

A job. It was a job. She tried to remind herself. It didn't feel like a simple job. More like an elaborate movie role with a script too complicated to remember and scenes too challenging for her meager acting skills.

And then there was Darias. Far too handsome. Warm, charming, kind. She was beginning to hope he'd do something awful and off-putting so she could squelch her very unwelcome and inconvenient attraction to him. Pretending to be madly in love with him was one thing—actually being in love with him would be a total disaster under the circumstances. She'd have only herself to blame if she grew attached to him and got her heart crushed when he sent her packing after one year.

So she tossed and turned until the cool fingers of morning light crept through her curtains like nosy neighbors.

A knock on the door made her sit upright in bed. Who would disturb her before it was even fully light out? "Hello?"

"It's Beatriz. May I come in?"

9

Emma jumped out of bed. "Hold on a moment." She rapidly ran a comb through her hair and splashed water on her face, as if that would make her seem like less of a fraud in Beatriz's eyes. She unlocked the door and opened it.

Darias's sister was elegantly dressed in a navy blue ensemble, her face made up and her hair in a neat bun. "Oh, you're not up yet." She glanced at Emma's pajamas.

"What time is it?"

"Ten to ten."

"Oh, goodness. The wedding dress appointment. I had no idea it was so late. I guess it's only two A.M. in New York right now."

"Don't worry. I already called them, and they're going to bring a big selection of dresses to the palace at noon." Beatriz came in and closed the door behind her. "It's easier for Mama not to be out and about so much right now. People are whispering behind their hands."

Emma nodded, feeling rather cornered. "I'm so sorry to hear about what happened. Very shocking."

"Almost as shocking as the news that my twin brother is about to marry someone he's never mentioned to any of us before."

Perhaps it was a good time to be honest. Just a little bit honest. "The need for him to be married in order to take the throne precipitated things. I'm not sure he'd even thought about marrying me until that happened."

Beatriz scrutinized her with deep brown eyes not unlike her brother's. "I'd imagine so. It's a lot of pressure. On you, too." She cocked her head, as if looking for a reaction.

"It was a surprise when he proposed. I admit that he had to talk me into it." Boy, was that ever true.

One of Beatriz eyebrows lifted. "You weren't sure if you wanted to marry him?"

Emma inhaled, gathering her thoughts. This was dangerous territory. "It's a lot of responsibility, to be the wife of a king. I'm just an elementary school teacher. I'm from a very ordinary background. It's all rather intimidating to me."

Beatriz nodded, obviously taking this in. "I understand. There's a lot to learn—palace etiquette, how to interact with the public. This life allows some luxuries, but it's a full-time job representing the royal family. I suppose you were right to be wary." Her mouth tilted into a small smile. "I'll help you in any way I can. Feel free to ask me questions about things that confuse you."

Did she really now have an ally, rather than a suspicious antagonist? It seemed too much to hope for.

"Darias has had a lot of women pursue him over the years. In general they're far more interested in the prospect of a luxurious lifestyle and access to the Altaleone jewels than in my brother's heart and soul. As his sister, it's made me wary."

"I can imagine. I'm sure you deal with the same kind of thing yourself."

Beatriz frowned, looking almost confused. "Hardly. I'm never going to be queen."

Emma found it hard to believe she didn't still have suitors anxious to enjoy a well-feathered royal life. Maybe men were intimidated by Beatriz and the prospect of life among royals.

She wanted to assure Beatriz that she wasn't marrying Darias for his money or connections, but that would have been an outright lie. Better to keep quiet. "I want to do my best to help Darias fulfill his duties to his family and the country." Now, that was true. No need for Beatriz to know she was being paid for it.

To her surprise Beatriz clasped her hands. "You have no idea how relieved I am to hear that." Beatriz hands were cold. Cold hands, warm heart? She couldn't tell. "The most important thing right now is to help Mama through this nightmare." Her big brown eyes moistened. "It's really too much for her to bear. It's not fair that she had to find them as well as deal with being left alone after a thirty-year marriage. I'm doing everything I can think of to keep things calm and smooth for her. Honestly, Darias turning up with you is the only thing that's made her smile since she found the bodies. It seems like a year ago but it was barely ten days."

Emma shivered. "Her grief is so raw. I lost my mom last year, and some mornings I still wake up and can't believe it."

Beatriz squeezed her hands. "I'm so sorry." Her sympathy seemed totally genuine and Emma felt a flood of emotion and guilt at continuing to deceive her. "My father and I didn't always see eye to eye, and I wish I could go back in time and change some of the things I said." Her face was pale. "I can't tell Mama that, of course."

Emma nodded, feeling compassion. She realized that Darias's sister was desperate to talk to someone about her pain. Even someone she barely knew and didn't entirely trust.

If she only knew.

"Well, as I said, the most important thing is to keep things ticking along smoothly." She leaned in, suddenly very close. "Mama had a nervous breakdown many years ago. She lost a baby late in the pregnancy and took it very hard. I was only a child, but I remember being very scared. There have been moments lately when I wonder if it's about to happen again." She gripped Emma's hand. "Don't tell anyone I told you that."

"Of course not," said Emma quickly. "And I'll do everything I can to keep her calm and steady."

Beatriz stood up suddenly. "You'd better get ready for the fitting. Pin your hair up. It'll be easier to see the necklines."

Emma felt her long hair sprawling over her shoulders. "Good idea."

Beatriz shot her one more long, hard look, studying her, as if trying to decide whether she was someone she could trust, or not. "And don't tell Darias I spoke to you."

When Emma came downstairs, feeling self-conscious with her hair pinned in a wedding-y style, Darias was talking to his mom and Beatriz.

"Good morning, my love." His deep voice—and those words—awoke something inside her.

"Morning." Her voice cracked. She froze as Darias walked toward her. *Relax. Act natural. He's supposed to be your longtime boyfriend.*

He slid his arms around her waist and lowered his lips to hers. The kiss was quick, nothing more than a soft peck, really, but it left her gasping for breath, with heat rising up her neck to her cheeks.

"I'm going to meet with a long line of lawyers and accountants in Casteleone. Hopefully, they can fill me in on all the details my father and grandmother never had a chance to tell me."

She managed a shaky smile as they stepped apart. "Is there any kind of dress you like best?"

"Any dress with you in it."

If she didn't know better, she'd think that playful smile easing across his bold mouth was utterly genuine.

She did know better, though. "I think that between the three of us we'll find something you'll like."

"But he must absolutely not see it until your wedding day," called his mom, scolding and excited at the same time.

"Of course not, Mama. I intend to uphold every outdated and silly tradition in Altaleone, whether I believe in it or not."

She looked warmly at her son and smiled. "I know you're just teasing me."

"You may think I'm joking, Mama, but I truly do

intend to do my best to uphold all my responsibilities as king and as the head of the family."

Emma snuck a look at Beatriz, who should have every right to the same responsibilities as Darias. Beatriz raised a brow. "And I will do my best to make sure your bride is radiant and relaxed on her wedding day."

The dresses were breathtaking. She tried on a range of styles, from simple fitted satin gowns to frothy concoctions with crystal beaded bodices. Darias's mom cried at least four times. "I just love weddings," she exclaimed. "Since none of my daughters have married yet, this is my first time to fuss over one."

Emma preferred the simple dresses without much ornamentation, but they agreed that something with a bit more oomph would look better in video footage and photos of the wedding. They settled on a full-skirted gown with a fitted bodice piped with tiny seed pearls, and a long veil hemmed with matching tiny pearls.

The next few days where a whirlwind of consultations with party planners, hair dressers, personal shoppers, photographers and assorted other people, most of whom spoke very good English. Darias was gone nearly all day every day, presumably getting up to speed on the financial and political responsibilities of the monarchy.

In some ways it was a relief not to be around him, given the unsettling effect he'd started to have on her, but she hated the responsibility of answering so many questions without him there. Luckily, people weren't bold enough to ask very personal questions like how they'd met. When they asked other tricky questions, like what was Darias's favorite gemstone or which pattern of plate would he prefer, she could honestly answer that she really wasn't sure.

Most nights she was so exhausted that she slept like the dead and didn't even worry about palace ghosts or midnight visitors. She could sleep easy knowing that—so far—she'd done her part to uphold her bargain with Darias, and a call to New York had confirmed that her brother was still safely ensconced at The Fountains.

As the wedding day approached, Darias's younger siblings started to arrive from near and far, all of them seemingly pleased to meet her. They all seemed warm and charming, despite the slightly awkward moment.

"You don't speak Italian or German?" Darias's younger sister Callista had long, chestnut curls and hypnotic jade-green eyes. They were sitting next to each other at dinner the night before the wedding, and everyone had nearly finished a very rich chocolate cake for dessert. "French?"

"I'm afraid not."

Callista blinked in amazement. "Where did you go to school?"

"Just the local schools. In New Jersey."

"The public schools? The free ones?" She looked shocked. "Were your parents socialists or something?"

"Something like that." Emma wanted to laugh. These people lived in such an alternate universe. "I still managed to graduate from college."

"Princeton? I went for a tour of it with my father

after I got in." Her big eyes suddenly filled with tears. "Damn it. I keep forgetting."

"I'm so sorry about what happened."

"I just can't believe he's gone. He planned to visit me in Paris next month." Callista let out a deep sigh, then lifted her chin. "Princeton's a wonderful school, though. I might have gone there if I didn't get into MIT."

"I didn't go to Princeton." No need to make this charade any more elaborate than it already was. "I went to Rutgers."

"Oh."

"You're not hassling my fiancée are you, Calli?" Darias leaned over.

"Just wondering why she doesn't speak any languages at all." She winked at Emma. "Except presumably the language of love."

"Watch yourself, sis. You're not too old for me to strap you to a chair with zip ties again."

"Can you believe that?" Callista raised a brow at Emma. "You want to watch this one. He's too creative for his own good sometimes."

Darias's mother stood up. "Darlings, you know it warms my heart to have you all here, but I think we should get some sleep. We all have a long day tomorrow and need to look presentable for the cameras."

Emma swallowed. She'd forgotten about all the reporters that would be here. Tomorrow her picture would be splashed all over the press and the Internet and she'd go from total obscurity to a familiar face, at least in Europe.

Luckily in America no one cared much about European monarchs—especially from obscure microstates—so she wasn't likely to become notorious there. Unless something went horribly wrong.

Which it wouldn't.

Not if she could help it.

Emma was already awake the next morning when Beatriz knocked on her door. Darias's twin sister had clearly assigned herself the task of making sure all aspects of the wedding went smoothly. It was a little oppressive to have someone breathing down her neck under the circumstances, but helpful to have someone assist her through the arduous process of turning into a royal bride.

Her hair was straightened, then curled again into long, loose waves, then pinned into an elegant updo. She probably hadn't spent that much time on her hair in the last year. A makeup artist spent forty-five minutes making her look like an airbrushed version of herself, and the dressmaker fussed over the gown, putting stitches into strange places to ensure an absolutely perfect fit.

"You do look the part." Beatriz's cool comment, said with a totally straight face, almost made Emma wonder if she knew more than she let on. Or maybe all the Leones just spoke this way. Keeping up appearances was probably an important part of royal life. "No one would suspect that you don't have a drop of royal blood."

Now Emma blinked. "Am I supposed to?"

"It is traditional for royals to marry someone who is at least a member of the aristocracy somewhere. I suppose it's a shame you aren't a Kennedy."

"They're all cursed. I'd rather just be me."

Beatriz smiled. "Very sensible." To Emma's surprise she leaned in and kissed her on both cheeks. "At three o'clock today you will officially be royal, anyway."

The ceremony would take place at Casteleone Cathedral, in the center of town, and Emma traveled there—alone—in a gilded coach pulled by four gleaming white horses with blue feathers on their heads. There was an alarming moment when one of the horses spooked at a camera flash, but the coachman soon got things under control and they continued a slow parade through the crowd.

Beatriz and her mom had shown her how to wave, and she waved and smiled at the crowd, wondering what on earth the people thought of this strange foreign girl swooping in to marry their gorgeous and eligible young monarch.

When the carriage pulled up in front of the grand Gothic cathedral, she was helped from it by two footmen in gold brocade. Little girls in striped dresses strewed rose petals on the ground in front of her as she walked toward the main door, with two older girls carrying the long train of her veil.

This was *crazy*.

She couldn't say she'd spent years dreaming of her wedding day and planning every detail, but she certainly never thought it would be like this. Not so much the pomp and ceremony, but the grim reality that she was marrying a virtual stranger as part of a neat business arrangement.

She could never have done this if her parents were alive. Her mom would have kept her honest.

An older male family member had been drummed up to give her away, and he arrived gleaming with medals in a ceremonial uniform. He didn't speak but took her hand and guided her up the steps to the cathedral doors.

Emotion suddenly clogged the back of her throat. If her dad were alive would he even have given her away? Or would he have still been too busy touring with his band or losing himself in drugs? They reached the door of the church, and a thousand faces turned to stare from the pews.

She managed to keep a shaky smile on her face. Not too beaming, though. She didn't want to look fake. Even though she was.

Organ music boomed over them and she scanned the altar end of the cathedral for Darias, who was waiting in the wings somewhere, along with his brother Rigo, the best man.

Just keep it together.

Her stand-in father walked her down the aisle so slowly she began to wonder if they'd ever get there. One of the little flower girls started sneezing, and Emma welcomed the opportunity to fuss over her and ease the crushing sense of formality.

Her dread grew as they reached the altar. *This is it. You're going to stand up before all these people, and God, and lie to them. Until death us do part.*

Or not.

Where was Darias? She tried to scan the space as surreptitiously as possible. Maybe he decided to back out. She'd be left alone in front of all these people, to suffer under their pitying stares.

The she saw him. Her heart squeezed at the sight

of him. He looked so tall and dashing in the ceremonial uniform, black with a red collar and cuffs, gold brocade slashing across his chest. He looked every bit the handsome prince from a fairy tale.

Except this was no fairy tale. The organ music swelled to a close, and the murmur of conversation hushed to a grim silence. Darias walked toward her, expression serious, eyes hooded and mouth set in a grim line.

As he drew close their eyes met and a jolt of energy flashed between them. What was he thinking right now? Did he wish this was a true marriage with the promise of a lifetime of love?

Her chest tightened. How different things would be if it was.

Her elderly companion slid his arm from hers, and Darias took her hand. She tried not to notice how her skin responded to the heat of his fingers. It took all her concentration to keep her expression neutral and pleasant as they walked the last few steps toward the altar, where the officiant waited.

She could feel her heart beating a hundred miles an hour inside the tight bodice of her dress, as the officiant uttered the words she'd rehearsed with Beatriz. They were in the local language but similar to the weddings she'd attended back home, so she tried her best to follow their meaning until they reached the part where she'd have to respond.

At last it came. She tried to clear her throat silently, hoping she wouldn't croak or squawk like a chicken as she said "I do" in the unfamiliar tongue.

Darias slid the ring on her finger. The size of the diamond, ringed with yet more diamonds, made it look fake. Unlike everything else happening here, she knew it was real.

The officiant murmured more words, looking at Darias, and he said "I do," as well, before they were officially pronounced man and wife. Just like in the U.S., it was now time for the new husband to kiss his bride.

She held her breath as his sensual mouth moved toward hers. Pictures of this moment would probably ricochet around the world so she needed it to look warm and genuine.

Pretend it's real. Pretend you know him and love him.

Her lips met his and warmth exploded in her chest as they kissed.

If only it were real.

The scent of him tormented her and for a second she felt a tantalizing hint of tongue, but then he pulled back, eyes dark.

She shivered slightly, trying to get herself under control. The officiant continued talking, then the organ music started up again, and Darias slid his arm through hers and led her back toward the doors. Soon they were outside, blinking in the bright sun, as cameras flashed and the waiting crowd cheered.

Darias leaned in. "Thank you."

His whisper heated her ear. She couldn't think of an appropriate response so she kept her smile in place and waved as she'd been taught. After an eternity of photo ops, they climbed into a different carriage—the horses had red plumes—

that took them back to the palace, where a celebration feast was arranged.

"Are all the people from the town going to come to the palace?"

"Oh, no. There's a feast laid on for them in the town square. This is for friends, family, international dignitaries."

"Will I have to mingle?"

"I'm afraid so, but I'll be right with you. Just nod and smile. You're doing an amazing job. My mom has been glowing all morning. After recent events that's a huge blessing." He squeezed her hand, blissfully unaware of the alarming effect he had on her. "Just a few more hours and we can relax in private."

That's what I'm afraid of.

10

Emma stayed away from the champagne during the afternoon and evening of feasting and celebrating. She was a lightweight at the best of times and wanted to make sure she didn't do anything foolish.

Finally at midnight Darias rang a spoon against a glass. The din of noise slowly subsided as one by one, people turned to look at him. "Thank you all for coming to celebrate my wedding. My bride and I will be retiring to enjoy our wedding night. Please stay until dawn and enjoy our hospitality."

The announcement sounded like something from the fourteenth century, like many of the day's events. He held out his hand regally, and she took it with as much of a smile as she could muster.

This is it.

How would they sleep in the same bed? The palace was far too populated with family and staff—not to mention all the guests sleeping there that night—for them to do anything but share a bed.

She walked from the room on Darias's arm, waving and accepting compliments from a hundred strangers on what should have been the most magical and romantic day of her life. Not a hollow mockery of it.

"Thanks," she whispered to Darias. "I was getting really tired." Now, though, adrenaline sparked through her.

"That much socializing takes its toll. I half wish I could go up into the attic and paint for the rest of the night. That's my favorite way of coming down from too much excitement."

"You could."

He laughed. "Hardly. At least these days no one will be waiting outside our door to see bloodied sheets as evidence of your virginity being taken, but if I spent the night painting they'll start whispering that I'm gay or something."

"Are you?" Oddly, the thought hadn't occurred to her before. If he was gay, it would make perfect sense why he needed to buy a bride rather than just fall in love with one.

And what a relief that would be. She'd soon stop harboring foolish feelings for a man who didn't even like women.

"No. I adore women."

"As I suspected." He said it with such conviction that she had to smile. "I suppose that's why you couldn't settle on just one."

"Indeed." The hint of apology in his tone combined with the sparkle in his warm, brown eyes to make his confession rather adorable. Even though he was all but admitting that he'd made their arrangement so he could continue his pursuit of all the fabulous women out there rather than getting stuck with one "until death us do part," as they'd promised earlier. Or at least she thought they did. It was hard to tell what with the local dialect.

They climbed the stairs to the second floor, under his painted ancestors' stern gaze, her holding up her voluminous skirt. She knew where his bedroom was, though she'd never been inside it. "I should stop by my room and get my toothbrush."

"No need. The staff have brought all your effects to our room."

"Oh." She froze. She'd left the contract on top of the wardrobe. Could anyone have found it up there? Should she tell Darias or would he be furious with her for being so careless? "Can I just pass by my old room to make sure nothing got left behind?"

He shrugged. "Okay."

But the door was now locked—she'd left it unlocked—and she didn't have her key. She'd have to sneak in some time tomorrow to retrieve it. If it was still there.

If it wasn't....

She rattled the handle. "I'm not sure I like having someone just pick up my stuff and move it. Some things are private."

"I feel the same way. Why do you think I stayed in New York for so long?" His wry grin warmed her heart. "You get used to it, though. Having no privacy."

"I guess marriage is somewhat similar. You get used to sharing your life with someone." His silence made her regret her words. "In a real marriage, of course," she whispered. "We'll do our best to honor each other's privacy."

"Naturally."

They abandoned their efforts to enter her room—she certainly wouldn't be able to retrieve the contract and walk out with it in the presence of staff—and headed for his.

See? She could talk to him in a businesslike fashion. She'd even got used to the sight of him in gold brocade and with that stiff collar accenting the hard lines of his jaw.

His room was unlocked, and he held the door open for her. "Oh, goodness," she said, as she entered and saw the room bedecked with vases of white and yellow flowers. "Are these a tradition?"

"The white ones represent the purity of the bride," he said with a mischievous grin.

"And the yellow?"

"The treasure of love."

She grimaced. "I hope this place isn't haunted. The ghosts will know what we're up to."

Darias put a finger to his lips. He pointed to the ceiling, then the bedside tables.

"What?" She tried to figure out what he was pointing to.

He pulled his phone from his pocket and started tapping.

"Are you texting the ghosts?"

He held the phone up. He'd typed: **Might be bugged. Be careful.**

"Oh, you're just texting the friend who missed his plane," she said, to cover, nodding. "Tell him we miss him."

Darias winked and smiled, which made heat rise inside her.

Then a weird thought occurred to her. She leaned

in until her lips almost touched his ear. "Is it safe to whisper?" She could barely hear her own voice.

He nodded. "And I'll ask Gibran to have the room swept for bugs tomorrow, but during the wedding the staff were so busy that there was just too much opportunity for someone with connections to get in here. I need to get a guard posted here."

His breath heated her neck. "Let's get into bed. It will be easier to talk under the covers," he whispered.

Great. Now they had to be up close and personal whether they wanted to or not.

Either that or not talk. Which would be weird.

She found her clothes in one of the two ornate mahogany wardrobes and pulled out a pair of white cotton pajamas. "Sweetie, could you help me out of this dress?"

Might as well make it sound convincing.

"Or course, my love. You looked radiant."

She giggled. This sounded so fake. She could feel his strong hands on the zipper, and it made her lightheaded. "Did I tell you that I'm a virgin?"

His hands stopped. "Of course. I couldn't marry you if you weren't. Altaleone tradition forbids it." She could hear the teasing in his voice as he played along.

"I know. I've been saving myself." It was hard not to laugh. Not that she really was all that experienced, anyway. "I do hope you'll be gentle with me."

To her surprise he suddenly slid warm fingers inside the waistband of her dress. She gasped, and her belly contracted. "I hope I can control myself enough for that."

His touch sent heat rushing to her core. "You'd better try." She batted at his hands.

He slid them out, his fingertips gliding sensually over her skin.

Okay, teasing him was a terrible idea. Now her body was about to burst into flames, and he was sliding her dress down over her shoulders.

"I can do it."

"On our wedding night? I think not." His low voice was sensual and suggestive. No doubt he was just playing along with their charade.

Or maybe he did expect to have sex with her. He'd paid her a lot of money, after all. He'd take her pretend virginity, then proceed to embark on affairs with other women, like princes and kings before him had done for centuries.

He must have felt her stiffen. He leaned in and again she felt his breath hot on her ear. "I'm only teasing. Your virginity is safe with me."

"I'm not really a virgin."

"I know." His throaty whisper made her feel less virginal than ever.

She needed to figure out how to get the dress off and her pajamas on, preferably without stripping naked in front of him. Especially with her nipples tight with arousal from all the unwanted touching.

"I'm going to brush my teeth." He must have heard her thoughts.

Houdini probably couldn't have got out of that dress and into the pajamas any faster than she did. She put the dress on a hanger, its big skirt pooling out of the closet and onto the floor, then climbed into bed and pulled the covers up under her chin.

Darias emerged dressed only in a towel, and she averted her eyes from the tanned expanse of his muscled torso. "Hey, that's my side."

"Not anymore. I can only sleep on the left."

"Me, too."

"Guess we'll have to share." Why couldn't she stop teasing him? It helped to lighten the tension. And newlyweds bickering over silly things was probably more realistic than them declaring their undying love for each other.

She looked up at the burgundy curtains hanging around the bed, the gold brocade walls and an extravagantly framed collection of pictures of hunting dogs—anywhere but at his damp, towel-clad body.

"This bedroom is just your style," she joked.

"Isn't it, though? All I need is a powdered wig, and I'll fit right in."

"I guess you were born knowing you'd have to live like this."

"It's a tough job but someone's got to do it." He locked the bedroom door. "This room has beautiful features if you strip away all the excess," he pointed to the gorgeous inlaid wood ceiling. "But I'm not going to suggest any redecorating until my mom has had a long time to recover. She's endured too much change already."

"I think it's wonderful that you care so much about your mom's feelings."

"She deserves it. She's a wonderful woman." The sincerity in his voice touched her. "I'd do anything for her."

She averted her eyes as he climbed under the covers and switched out the lamp on the bedside table. The room was dark but not completely, and her eyes began to adjust to make out his bold features. His weight on the mattress tilted her slightly toward him. His body heat seemed to creep toward her under the covers, stirring something inside her.

Oh, dear. And now they had to produce some kind of audio performance in case someone was listening. "You will be gentle with me, since it's my first time?" She tapped her ear, to make her purpose clear.

"Of course I will, my love. Though it will be hard to control my passions when I've forced myself to keep my hands off you for so long." Mischief danced in his eyes, even in the darkness. He leaned in to whisper. "Let's do some visual effects in case there's a camera."

Her eyes widened. There had damn well better not be a camera. She just stripped naked in front of it. And before she'd even had time to give an answer, Darias zeroed in for a pretend kiss.

Except that it wasn't pretend. Once again his lips touched hers, soft and tender, and it was all she could do not to kiss him back. Her nipples thickened again and her thighs shivered. How could he do this without becoming aroused?

Not that she could tell, really. He managed to artfully keep any telltale parts of his body away from her.

Now his arm slipped around her waist. "Finally, we're man and wife."

Her lips tingled, wanting to kiss his again. Which was not at all how this should be going!

"Yes, the wedding was lovely. Your family has

been so welcoming." *I wonder how they'll talk about me right after I disappear in one year's time.* "I don't know what I would have done without Beatriz."

Darias frowned. His eyes met hers for a second, and she got a feeling he wanted to say something but checked himself at the last minute. "Yes, she's very loyal to the family. She wanted to be sure everything happened without a hitch. I'm grateful to her."

She heard a hint of warning in his voice. One that echoed her own instincts. She had a feeling Beatriz was being so helpful on the "keep your friends close and your enemies closer" principle.

His arm still rested on her waist, holding her so that only a few warm inches of air separated their torsos. Exquisite torture. And what if someone was watching? She pulled her arm from beneath the covers and lifted it to cup his cheek and stroke his hair, like a lover might.

At first he looked confused, then he submitted himself to her caresses with a bemused expression, until he leaned in, pressed his mouth to her neck and rasped, "Let's make love."

11

To say it was awkward to "make love" to Darias while he propped himself on his elbows and moved his hips over her, under the covers, would be the understatement of the century.

For a start, she could definitely feel how aroused he was. He tried to keep his hips raised enough so as not to touch her, but every now and then she could feel the hard length of his manhood brush against her thighs or belly.

The sensation made her catch her breath, which probably made the sound effects more realistic. She kept her arms wrapped around his neck, fingers playing in the hair at the nape of his neck. It was a good thing she got to keep her eyes closed.

Darias built the rhythm to a crescendo, then emitted a groan and collapsed to the side of her. He leaned his face in so close that his lips were touching her ear. "I just want you to know that if I was really making love to you, it would be a lot longer and more passionate."

"You don't have to prove anything to me," she whispered back. Then she said louder. "That was amazing."

Darias tried to hide the smile crossing his mouth. She could tell he wanted to laugh. The whole situation was so tense and crazy. Both of their bodies zinging with arousal, writhing around under the covers and pretending to make love rather than actually doing it.

"We could really do it, you know." He gazed at her through narrowed eyes, still whispering.

She blinked and swallowed. "I don't think that's a good idea."

He relaxed his head into the pillow. "As you wish."

She didn't wish. She'd love to touch all over his hard body and really let herself fall deep into one of those hesitant kisses.

But she knew that would be a disastrous. This was a game to Darias. A convenient arrangement with a finite end. Much better to keep her heart, and her private parts, tightly under wraps for the duration.

They rolled apart, heads each on their own pillow. Much better. They'd put on enough of a show to allay suspicion and possibly disappoint any eager viewers. After tomorrow the room would be cleared and they wouldn't have to fake it again.

How funny that she'd heard Darias fake an orgasm. There couldn't be many women who'd had that privilege. She couldn't imagine there were many women who'd lain in bed with him and willingly kept their hands to themselves, either.

This would be a lot easier if he were unattractive. Or a jerk.

Darias watched her, dark eyes gleaming.

She wondered if he intended to say something for any potential eavesdroppers. "I love you," perhaps. What else would real newlyweds whisper as they lay in bed together on their wedding night?

Sometimes it was hard to remember this was all fake. There was something magical about being folded into the bosom of this big family, when she was still reeling from the loss of her mom.

"You're a very special woman." His voice was low enough to be almost a conspiratorial whisper but probably loud enough to be picked up by recording equipment. Was he truly saying this to her, or was it for the benefit of snoopers?

"Thanks." Did it really matter whether he meant it or not? He was paying her handsomely to be here, and she needed to do her job.

It would get easier over time, wouldn't it?

At dawn Darias turned the shower as cold as possible. Last night had been almost unbearable torture. How was he supposed to lie in bed next to such a beautiful woman and not make love to her? Worse yet, he had to pretend to make love to her. Perhaps that hadn't been such a great idea. They didn't know for sure that someone was bugging the room, and they could have just pretended to be too tired. Probably many couples didn't make love on their wedding night after an exhausting day of festivities and too much booze.

But that idea appalled him. If he married a woman, he wanted her satisfied and filled with joy on her wedding night. Was he so narcissistic that he expected his paid wife to fake such delight?

He let out a dark sigh. Better that he get away from her and get on with the job of finding the enemy in their midst before something bad happened.

He turned off the shower and roughly toweled himself dry, then dressed in pants and a shirt, ready to greet the guests who'd stayed overnight, then make his excuses.

Emma looked like an angel with her gold hair splayed on the pillow. A sad angel. What lovely woman wanted her wedding to be a sham? His heart ached that he'd done that to her.

"I'm going to find Gibran and make sure the room is swept today—and every day."

There was no way he could pretend to make love to her again. It had half killed him. He couldn't be sure he could control himself the next time.

"Okay. I'll go find your mom and Beatriz and join them for breakfast."

"Perfect." She knew her job, and she performed it perfectly. Why did that make him feel like such a heel?

The next few days where a whirlwind of activity for Emma. A number of guests stayed at the palace after the wedding, including all of Darias's siblings. She was swept into a number of activities, including bicycle rides through the countryside, dining out in little pastry shops and cafes, and exploring the tiny villages that dotted the hillsides. They also played tennis on two courts behind the palace and rowed on a beautiful lake, and she watched his siblings jump their magnificent horses in a sand arena near the palace stables.

It was like living in a fairy tale—and knowing you're the bad fairy who shouldn't be there. She tried not to dwell on that, though. She figured she should make the most of this once-in-a-lifetime chance to immerse herself in the culture and customs of Altaleone, and enjoy what was really a long vacation in a billionaire's playground.

Nights, however, were a whole different story.

Darias was gone much of each day doing who knows what. It wasn't her business to ask. In the evenings he joined the family for dinner, and they all spent time chatting or watching a movie in the palace theater. Then they retired to their bedroom, where their conversation was so formal you might almost think they were being recorded. Except that he assured her they weren't.

"How was your day?" She never asked for details as they lay next to each other in bed, at least a foot of cool mattress in between their bodies.

"Fine. I met with the minister of agriculture. Learned about the grape harvest and how I can grow the market for our wine internationally." He never really gave details.

"Nice."

"Yes. Interesting."

His coronation was only three days away, and she knew he wanted to be up to speed on all his official and unofficial duties beforehand. Still, did it really take all day, every day?

Or was he avoiding her?

That was what it felt like.

Maybe he was carrying on with a different woman every afternoon? She couldn't smell them on him and saw no traces of lipstick on his cheek. Then was ashamed of herself for looking.

You're not really married. It's a sham.

She didn't believe it, though. They'd gone through the ceremony, and in her heart she wanted to be faithful and true to him at least for that one year.

But there'd been no clause in the contract about his behavior. Only about hers.

"What are you doing tomorrow?" It would be nice to go for a bike ride in the country with Darias. Or row on the lake with him.

"Meeting with the minister for exports and tariffs. There's a lot to learn about our trade relationships with other countries."

"Oh."

"Good night." His dark eyes met hers for a brief moment, and she wondered if any thoughts about her flashed behind them.

"Good night." Sleeping next to him was torture. Sometimes she lay awake for hours, willing herself to be completely still. She could hear his soft breathing and feel the weight of his body shifting on the mattress. His subtle masculine scent tormented her, lingering on the sheets even when he wasn't there.

"Only two more days until the coronation!" Darias's mom was busy with Beatriz, talking to florists and briefing the staff. Emma wondered how she'd manage when all the festivities were over and she had less to distract her from her loss. Right now they were sitting at the big dining table going over details for the coronation dinner. "And my sister is finally able to get away for a few days."

"Aunt Liesel?" Beatriz sounded shocked.

"Yes. She hasn't been here in years."

"Because daddy couldn't stand her." Beatriz frowned. "Are you sure that's a good idea? She's such a pot stirrer."

"Beatriz! Mind your tongue. She's my only sister. The only member of my family that I have left now." She pulled a tissue from her sleeve and blew her nose. "I've been talking to her on the phone every day since your father died, and I'm very much looking forward to seeing her."

Beatriz grimaced. "Does Darias know?" As usual Darias was off on official business somewhere.

"Not yet, but I'm sure he'll be happy to see his aunt."

"Don't count on it. Goodness, look at all this mail." A staffer had brought in a tray piled with envelopes. "I suppose it's probably just thank you letters from wedding guests. Emma, would you mind sorting through it and dealing with the letters for Darias?"

"Sure." She was glad of something to do. She felt at a loose end a lot of the time. She started to organize the letters into stacks. Most of them were for Darias's mom, Her Royal Highness Carolina Leone, but a few were for other siblings and several were addressed to Darias.

"You can open them and respond. I'm sure he'd be grateful." Beatriz was drawing up the seating arrangements for the coronation banquet.

"Isn't it illegal to open someone else's mail?" The idea shocked her.

"Not in Altaleone. Besides, you're married. That

means you're pretty much the same person." Beatriz's lifted eyebrow left her unsure if this was a joke or a taunt. For all Beatriz's helpful intimacy, she still seemed a touch suspicious about the true nature of Emma's relationship with Darias.

"Okay. I guess. If you think he wouldn't mind."

"Oh, Darias thinks all this socializing business is nonsense. He'd rather be up in a garret with a paintbrush."

"Will he have time to paint, eventually, when things calm down?" It would be a terrible waste if such an interesting and committed artist got so busy with trade tariffs that he never painted again.

"Who knows?" Beatriz shrugged.

"Darias will do what Darias wants to do," said his mom. "He's been that way since the day he was born. We're just lucky that his loyalty to his family and country are at the top of the list. His father was so surprised that he made such a success of his art. Did you know that one of his paintings sold for seven hundred thousand dollars?"

"Yes." She smiled. "I worked at his gallery. I'm sure his gallery owner is hoping he'll find the time to keep painting."

"I thought you were a teacher?" Emma felt Beatriz steely gaze turn to her like a laser beam.

"I was. The gallery was a side job. I've always loved art." She tried to smile. No need to mention her desperate need for extra cash.

"I think it's wonderful, dear, that you have a passion for education and for art," said Darias's mom. "We'll have to makes sure those aren't wasted here in Altaleone. We have excellent schools in our country. We'll have to go on a tour of them soon."

"Great." More people she could leave in the lurch when she hit the tarmac a year from now. "I'd love to see how things here are different from the U.S."

She'd finished sorting the letters and spaced the piles out on the table for each person to grab. Quite a few were addressed to her and Darias, which felt totally weird even though it shouldn't. They were all standard notes congratulating them on their wedding, and she wrote the names on a list so she could send a note in return.

At last she was down to the letters for Darias. She felt uneasy ripping into an envelope addressed to someone else, but they did all have the slim appearance of routine thank you cards.

The first one, however, made her breath catch in her throat.

The queen is gone, her secrets kept
Her son so close behind her
The brave new heir does hope to rule
But battle brings the sound of thunder

She glanced up at Beatriz—busy with the seating plan—and her mother—looking at pictures of flower arrangements—and knew Darias would want her to go straight to him.

This was a threat of some sort but too vague to be useful. Maybe Gibran could find some clues in the card itself.

Damn, she got her fingerprints on it already. She tucked it back in the envelope and feigned a yawn.

"I'm just going to take these upstairs. I'll be back in a bit."

She hurried for the bedroom. The two staff members she passed on the way suddenly seemed like suspects. Everyone did. What if Beatriz was jealous of her twin brother inheriting and wanted him out of the way?

Her heart pounded as she closed the door behind her and locked it, then reached for her phone. Darias picked up right away, surprise in his voice. She knew better than to disturb him for no good reason. "Darias, something strange came in the mail. You need to see it, and Gibran."

"Where are you?"

"Our bedroom."

"Lock the door. Don't move. I'll be right there."

He'd hung up before she could protest that it wasn't actually a ticking time bomb. She should have said it was just a printed note.

Less than five minutes had passed when she heard a knock on the door. "It's me, Darias."

She opened it and he thrust in, expression grim, and placed his hands on her arms. "Are you okay?"

"Yes, it's just a letter." She nodded to where it lay on the bed. "But I didn't want to say anything to your mom. It's some kind of threat."

"I've called Gibran. He's on his way to meet us at the old castle. No one will overhear us there." He picked up the letter and scanned it, then tucked it into a pocket inside his jacket. "Let's go."

Her skin burned where his palms had left her upper arms. If he had any idea of her feelings for him, he'd think she was mad. How could her body even react like this when he might be in real danger?

Darias held the door for her, and she hurried along the corridor and down the stairs. "We're just heading out for a stroll," he called, as they passed the dining room, where his mom and Beatriz sat. "Do you want anything from town?"

Emma wanted to laugh. There were at least ten different staffers on hand to fetch anything they could dream of.

His mom smiled warmly at them, as if enchanted by young love's glow. "Enjoy your walk!"

They headed out into the blinding sunshine.

"You didn't even ask me what I found."

"Did it matter? Any kind of clue needs to be acted on immediately. I don't want to miss an opportunity to catch whoever did this."

They walked briskly down the long palace drive, out the wrought iron gates and onto one of the town's tree-lined, cobbled streets. Passersby smiled politely, clearly used to seeing the royals out and about. They rounded a corner and ascended a flight of steps up to the highest part of the town, where the old stone castle was clearly visible for miles around.

A guard in a blue uniform with gold brocade opened a door in the big iron gates and let them into the castle courtyard. For the first time she noticed there was a moat around the castle, with two swans gliding on its green surface. The tall wood doors opened before they got there, and another uniformed guard let them in.

Gibran waited in the dimly lit hallway, a grim expression on his chiseled features. Darias pulled the envelope from his jacket's inside pocket and handed it to Gibran without a word.

Gibran pulled out the paper gingerly, holding it between two fingertips. He read it, then frowned. "I think I know where this is from."

12

"You know who wrote it?" Darias's voice was gruff with urgency.

"Someone who knows medieval French literature. It's from an epic poem written by a little-known monk called LeBrec."

"And this is the exact wording?"

"More or less. A little is lost in translation to English. I suppose they wanted to make sure the message didn't get lost on someone without a command of medieval French."

"How do you recognize it?" Darias looked suspicious.

"I was educated at a very ancient French boarding school. This kind of thing was standard reading for us."

"I thought you were from the Middle East?"

Gibran shrugged. "It's a long story. I am the illegitimate son of a king who wished to be rid of me. I was also in the French foreign legion. But this note tells us a few things. It's written by someone educated, versed in history."

"Is it connected to the secret society, the Cross of Blood? I believe it has its roots in France."

"As does your family. The Leone line is descended from Charlemagne, king of the Franks."

"Yes, illegitimate descendants, like yourself. But he granted my ancestors the territory that became Altaleone."

"Your family has had many rivals over the centuries."

"Of course."

"Recently?"

"The days of broadswords and bloodshed are long over. Our rivals now are competitors in the fine wine industry and the diamond trade, or rival investors. My family has made most of its fortune in recent decades from speculative venture capital projects."

"Is there one rival that stands out?"

"There is one thorn in our side. The Aldobrando family has long laid claim to a large lake along our western border. Their argument holds no water, of course."

"Unlike the lake," Emma couldn't resist joking. This whole situation made her so tense she was almost shaking.

Both men turned to stare at her. Darias's stern expression softened into a smile. "Indeed. It's a beautiful lake, and I suspect they would like to develop it. Their estates lie close by but they lost access to the lake in the fifteenth century, when their ancestor paid it as a gambling debt."

Emma lifted her brows. "You'd think five centuries would be enough time to get over it."

Darias shook his head. "Five centuries is nothing to the aristocracy of Europe. And Lorenzo Aldobrando is a sharp-minded speculator. He's tried several times to obtain a lease on the old summer palace on the lake." Darias frowned, then stared hard at Emma. "Which—possibly not coincidentally—is the palace where the murders took place."

Gibran blew out.

Emma's brain raced. "Maybe he was hoping that the murders would destabilize the family and devalue the property enough that he could get it cheap, then possibly buy the land."

Darias shrugged. "That seems a bit drastic for a property investment."

"Is Aldobrando involved in this secret society?" asked Gibran

"I don't know yet, but I think we have our first real suspect."

Darias and Emma lay next to each other in bed that night, her alternately fretting about how to lay her hands on her contract with Darias and how to interpret the odd verse, and Darias poring over an age-stained nineteenth-century copy of the old French text that had been unearthed on a high shelf in the palace library. "But battle brings the sound of thunder. What the hell does that mean?"

"Cannons?"

"This was written in 1242. They didn't have cannons. At least I don't think so."

"Thundering hooves?"

Emma was trying to pick up some basic

French vocabulary by reading a language website on her phone. She felt very useless. And hated herself for noticing how powerful Darias's fingers were as they stroked the smooth pages of the old book. Did she have no conscience?

"Look at this." He beckoned her to come closer. She braced herself before leaning close enough to inhale his intoxicating scent. "The next line is something like, 'Distracted by a maiden fair, the king will lose his all.'" He frowned. "Okay, that doesn't really rhyme. I'm no linguist."

"Do you think the person who wrote that note intended you to read the book and see what happens?"

"Sure. Wouldn't anyone?" His brown eyes rested on hers. "A maiden fair." His mouth softened. "That's you."

She held herself stiffly a few inches from him, not wanting to be too rude when he needed her to see the book, but hoping he wouldn't sense her attraction.

"I do hope I'm not being a distraction to you."

"Well..." His soft gaze fell to her mouth. "I won't say my thoughts haven't wandered to consider all the things we haven't been doing."

She swallowed, as her lips responded to his stare. "They think you're distracted by being madly in love with me. Of course they couldn't be more wrong." She lifted her chin, hoping she sounded convincing. And why wouldn't she? She knew Darias wasn't in love with her and so did he.

"I think we've presented a very convincing front to the world. Enough to baffle my enemies." He laid the book on the covers and shifted so that his gorgeous bare torso turned toward her.

She shrank away from him a bit. It was hard not to look at his muscled chest. Why couldn't he wear a pajama top like he had before?

"Either you're a very good actress…" He lifted a hand and stroked her cheek. "Or you're as attracted to me as I am to you."

"I'm a terrible actress." She'd been trying to hide her feelings, not exaggerate them. Could he really see right though her? How embarrassing. "I'm just trying to do my job here and not overstep my bounds. I'm glad you think I've been doing okay."

"Okay? You've been magnificent. My whole family has fallen in love with you."

Except you.

"I'm not so sure that Beatriz loves me. I think she's still rather suspicious."

"That's her nature. She has my best interests at heart. But I don't want to talk about Beatriz." His hand still rested on her cheek, which now burned under its warmth. Her nipples thickened, and her heart beat so loud she could almost hear it. Adrenaline rushed through her, and she half wanted to leap from the bed and run from the room.

The other half of her wanted to—

Before she had time to finish her thought, Darias leaned in and kissed her firmly and forcefully on the lips.

Oh, no. The thought forced its way through her consciousness, as her body said, *Oh, yes,* and pushed itself into Darias's warm embrace.

She twisted toward him and her arms wove into his without her consent, pulling him close until her breasts bumped against his chest.

Oh, yes.

The kiss deepened, his tongue slipping gently inside her lips, sparking arousal that thrilled every inch of her. She could feel one of his big hands sliding over her torso, past her waist, to gently cup her backside under the sheet. Her skin sizzled under his claiming touch.

His chest rose against hers, as if he were drinking in the scent of her as he drew her tighter into his arms. Her fingers reached up into his thick, soft hair, touched the firm line of his jaw and traced the powerful curve of his shoulder.

Oh, no.

She felt her heart open with all the emotions she felt for this man who'd put his own needs and desires aside to fulfill his duty to his family and his country. She'd fallen half in love with him the day she met him and knew him only as a talented artist. What she'd seen and learned since had only made her fall harder.

This would burn like fire when he grew tired of her and moved on.

At last their lips parted enough for her to gasp for air and try to cool the fevered rush of desire flooding through her.

"Emma, my Emma. I had no idea what I was

getting myself into when I made my unromantic proposal to you." He inhaled deeply, pushing a lock of hair back from her shoulder. "I thought I was a man in control of my desires, but being so close to you—sharing a bed with you—has driven me half mad."

Me, too.

She didn't want to confess it. Better to keep her feelings to herself until she knew where this was going.

"I promised myself that I wouldn't seduce you. That I'd keep things calm and cool between us, but I'm only human and I've failed in my quest."

His eyes sparkled with familiar mischief. Obviously, he wasn't beating himself up too hard over his lapse. "I made the mistake of choosing a woman far too beautiful to be only a pretend lover."

His gaze roamed over her face, and she felt color rise to her cheeks under his warm appraisal. "I want to paint you."

She stared. Most men would say, "I want to make love to you." Darias wasn't most men. "Do you have painting supplies here?"

"Of course. I have a studio set up on the top floor." He took her hand, ready to tug her gently from beneath the sheets.

"Now? It's after midnight."

"An enchanted time."

Butterflies stirred in her stomach. Letting him paint her would be safer than letting him make love to her. At least until she got her mind in the right place and reminded herself that this kiss didn't mean he was falling in love with her.

He climbed from the bed, gorgeous in the half-light, and tugged on some clothes, then grabbed her silk robe and handed it to her.

"What if someone sees us?"

"What if they do? Would it be so strange for me to take my gorgeous wife up to my studio to immortalize her?"

His words tugged at something deep inside her. She had to remind herself that one kiss didn't mean theirs had suddenly become a real marriage. He'd married her to avoid a tiresome lifetime commitment.

He took her hand and led her along the dimly lit corridors. The palace was so quiet at this time of night, though she knew security guards stood outside.

Of course that would be no protection if the enemy was inside the palace.

The tall doorways and high sconces cast long shadows in the hallways, giving the whole scene a mysterious air. "Are you afraid of the killer?" She looked around her, wondering if it was foolish to wander around in the dark.

"Being afraid won't do me any good. I need to use my brain to unravel the mystery. Painting gives me my best moments of clarity."

They climbed a staircase she'd never seen before, up to the third floor, where silent hallways led them to another staircase. "I didn't realize the palace had more than three floors."

"The upper attic is hidden behind a parapet

wall and can't be seen from the outside. It used to be divided into fifty tiny servants' rooms. We don't need that many these days, because of washing machines and fridges and cars—plus staffers want to live in their own homes—so my mom had them knocked together into a big studio." At the top of the stairs he keyed in a code and a low doorway opened into darkness. Darias switched on the light to reveal a large, low-ceilinged space lined with half-finished canvases.

"How have you found time to paint?"

"I haven't. Some of these are from years ago."

She looked around at the canvases, several of them contained shadowy half-painted images of women. Her predecessors. She was only one in a long line of girls to grace Darias's canvases.

"Why don't you come sit on this chair?" A gilt chair, probably an eighteenth-century original, sat in the middle of the room. He pulled a sheet from a trunk and draped it over the chair. Which was good, as probably a number of naked women had sat on that brocade-covered seat.

"I suppose you want me to take my clothes off."

"Please." He was preoccupied with squeezing some paint onto an easel, as if he could care less whether she was naked or not.

She took off her robe and pajamas and placed them in an awkward pile on the floor, then sat gingerly—totally self-conscious—on the chair. "How would you like me to sit?"

"Whatever feels natural. No need to pose. You can move if you like. As you know, I am more interested in painting your essence than the angles and curves of your body."

"You're the only representational artist at Keane Moss. Usually, he's all about enigmatic installations and cryptic word art."

Darias laughed. "I know. Representational painting is very old fashioned. In-the-know people say I only get away with it because I'm a prince." He winked, sending a shimmer of heat to her core. "Perhaps they're right. I don't care."

"Your paintings are beautiful. When you paint women, they always look powerful and intriguing." That was intimidating to think about. She didn't feel very powerful or interesting.

"I just paint what I see. And if people want to buy them and hang them in their living rooms, that's fine with me." His self-deprecating expression was adorable. "I've always loved painting. It's my way of escaping into my own world, where no one expects anything of me."

"Even now that you're famous and people are waiting for your paintings?"

"All that goes right out of my head when I pick up a brush." He rolled up his shirt sleeves, revealing strong forearms. She blinked. The memory of that hot kiss made her lips tingle.

"You're lucky. I don't think many people have that kind of escape."

He flipped through a stack of stretched

canvases, pulled out a large one already washed with a ghostly gray-brown and fastened it to a big easel. He squeezed some dark paint onto a palette, pulled a brush from a big jar, then stood in front of the canvas and looked right at her.

His hot gaze traveled over her like a searchlight, making her nipples tighten and her skin shiver. "I'm feeling self-conscious," she admitted. She probably shouldn't talk. Maybe he needed to concentrate. It didn't seem fair that he wore clothes and she was naked. But if you took that thought further, it wasn't fair that he was a wealthy prince and she was—

She wasn't even sure anymore. Not a teacher. Not a student. Not even a daughter, now that her mom was gone. She was still sister to Jonas, the true reason she'd ended up here.

The canvas was angled so she could watch the deft movements of his hands across its surface, sketching the outlines of her body and shapes of the imaginary landscape he drew around her.

She wondered if this painting would end up on the wall of Keane Moss and whether her former boss would recognize her. It seemed presumptuous to suggest that. Maybe this one would just be buried in his archive.

"What do you dream of?" he asked, suddenly.

"Uh, I have a lot of anxiety dreams. I'm waiting for the PATH train and it's not coming, that kind of thing."

He laughed. "Not that kind of dream. What kinds of goals and aspirations do you have?"

She hesitated. "Well, I always wanted to be a teacher. I had some really good ones when I was young. I've dreamed of owning a house, but obviously I'm years away from that. I always wanted to travel, but honestly I never had any practical plans to do so. I was too busy working and saving and studying."

"And now you've traveled to another country." His dark gaze roamed over her body. "To live."

"I guess you never know what's around the corner. Well, unless you're born a prince and you grow up knowing you're going to be king and live in a palace." She tried to sound teasing.

"My dad was supposed to rule next. I had no plans to be back here so soon." His rueful expression tugged at her heart. "No one really knows what life has in store."

Especially when there's a murderer hiding somewhere in the shadows.

"Do you think the murderer wanted to lure you back here for some reason?"

"Certainly a possibility." He frowned, but his attention was on the painting. "I'm watching my back, along with all the armed guards we hired. I do wonder if the coronation will flush them out. Do they want me to be crowned king, or do they seek to prevent it?"

Anxiety spiked in her gut. She didn't want to admit that she was scared for him.

"Either way, I won't be hiding in the shadows. I welcome the opportunity to draw them out into the open."

Darias obviously liked to talk while he painted. They discussed art and music and shared their favorite movies, while he sketched and shaded. She couldn't see much of the image from where she sat, but she'd seen enough of his paintings—which, while representational, were fairly monotone and abstract—to imagine what it must look like.

He painted in a muscular style, with broad, bold sweeps, and she loved watching his body move.

He'd kissed her. She got a weird rush of sensation and emotion every time she thought of it. Would he kiss her again?

Probably. Darias wasn't a man to leave something half finished.

"It's four A.M.," he said, at last. "I think we should go back to bed."

Her insides quivered. Surely they wouldn't lie in bed, each firmly rooted on their side of the mattress, now that they'd shared that kiss and he'd sketched her naked form onto a huge canvas?

If they did, though, she resolved not to be too disappointed.

He lifted her robe off the floor and held it while she slid her arms in. Of course her nipples stood to attention in his presence. He tied the sash around her waist, then slid his arms around her. Heat flashed through her as he lowered his mouth to hers and kissed her with fierce intensity.

Colors and lights flashed behind her eyes while their tongues moved together.

"Damn, you have no idea how badly I've been wanting to do that."

"While you were painting me."

"And before." He stroked her cheek. "You have no idea how much self-control I've exercised over the past weeks."

Me, too. But she didn't dare admit it. Better to keep her feelings to herself so he didn't feel pressured. "It has been strange sleeping together but not touching."

"Let's sleep together touching tonight." His eyes were dark with passion. His hands roamed over her body through the thin robe. "If we can make it back to our room first. My personal situation is becoming explosive."

She glanced at his crotch and saw his erection straining against the zipper of his black jeans. A smile tugged at her mouth. There was something exciting about knowing she had this kind of effect on him. "We'd better hurry."

They left the studio, and he turned off the lights and locked the door. They crept back through the empty corridors, trying to keep their footfalls silent on the stairs and the shiny marble floors. Their stealthy movements made her nervous. "If someone sees us sneaking around like this, they might shoot first and ask questions later. We should probably be talking loudly," she whispered.

There was no need to hide their midnight tryst. If anything, it made their relationship more believable.

"Somehow it's sexier this way. And I want to

keep my painting of you private. For my eyes only." His eyes roved over her, sparking heat under her skin.

At last they reached the bedroom, and she was almost giggling with excitement and anticipation.

Until they opened the door.

13

A strange man bent over the bedside table on Emma's side of the bed. He spun as the door opened. Emma gasped as Darias sprang forward and tackled him, pushing him face-first into the bed and tugging his arms behind his back.

"What are you doing here?"

"Gibran sent me." The man spoke in French-accented English.

"He sent you to my bedroom?" Darias's tone sounded incredulous.

"I have to check on you every half hour on my monitor downstairs."

"A video monitor?" Darias's voice dropped an octave. Emma's eyes widened. Had their own security staff been spying on them?

"No! We have a heat sensor. It measures whether there's anyone in the room or not. That's all." Darias still held him in a tight grip. "When the heat sensor went off I came to make sure everything was okay. I found the door unlocked, and you gone."

"We've been gone for hours." Darias sneered. "If I'd been kidnapped, we'd be in Paris by now."

"Our security cameras located you upstairs."

"You have a camera in my studio?" Now Emma cringed. Had the staff seen her naked?

"No. Just in the stairwells."

"Where else?" Darias still held him tight.

"All the hallways, outside. Nowhere private, just enough cameras so that we know where everyone is at all times."

"And enough sensors so you know where they're not."

The man swallowed. "Yes."

"Then why were you peering at Emma's nightstand?"

"I was looking behind the mattress. That's where the sensor is."

"Tomorrow morning I want a full report of exactly where each and every recording device and sensor is in this palace. I don't like being surprised in my own bedroom. If your equipment is so sophisticated, how come you didn't know I was headed back?" Darias pushed him into the mattress. "How do I know you're who you say you are?"

"Call Gibran."

"At four A.M.? I'm sure he'd enjoy that." Finally, he pulled back, leaving the man panting into the mattress. "Get off my bed and out of my room. And don't forget about that report."

The guard staggered out the door. He was wearing one of the black security guard uniforms, but the black shirt and pants were barely distinguishable from the attire worn by half the wealthy hipsters who frequented Keane Moss.

Darias smoothed the wrinkles on the bed. "I'm sorry about that."

"Why? It's not your fault." Her heart still pounded, and for once it had little to do with Darias's fiery, dark gaze or bold masculine features. "I'm just glad he wasn't here to kill us."

Darias locked the door, then took her into his arms. She let out a sigh and realized she'd been holding her breath. His arms felt safe and warm. He kissed her softly on the lips and the tension left her body, replaced by liquid need.

Her arms wrapped around him, and her fingers rested on the firm muscle of his back. She could feel the strength he'd just used to pin and hold a trained security guard. His confidence and decisiveness were reassuring.

And, as usual, he smelled great. She drank in his scent and let it soothe her, resting her cheek on his shoulder. She couldn't lie to herself—being intimate with Darias felt amazing, and for once they weren't putting on a show for anyone.

His hands slid up and down her back, caressing gently, stirring sensation beneath the skin. When he kissed her again, the heat of desire burned away the last traces of fear and her body softened in his arms.

I want to make love with him.

She acknowledged her thought. It was probably a bad idea, but she'd climbed onto this roller coaster ride. Once the car began going up that incline, there really was no other way out....

His fingers slipped under her robe, and her belly quivered. She'd stayed calm and still under his steady black gaze, but now she itched to move against him. She pushed her thickened nipples into his chest. She could feel his hardness against her and knew he was as aroused as her.

"Wait." His voice, thick with desire, drew her out of her lust-fogged stupor. "Heat sensor? I don't trust them. I want the room swept again—by my own trusted staff—before I'll risk being intimate with you in here."

No! She wasn't sure she could stand waiting. "We could be really quiet." She whispered it as if to prove her point.

"There might be video cameras. It's not worth taking a chance. If I have enemies out to ruin my family name, they could do anything with the images." His ragged breath heated her neck, and she could hear the pain in his voice. "Tomorrow we'll head out into the countryside, where no one will find us. No one will be able to watch us or hear us or track the heat of our bodies with high-tech equipment."

"My body might short circuit their equipment if I get into bed right now." She couldn't bring herself to pull away from him. "Too much heat."

He chuckled, his expression pained. "I hear you. I'm going to need a very cold shower to get even one wink of sleep tonight."

Darias let her go in the shower first, perhaps afraid things might get out of hand if he joined her. She let the cold water run over her fevered flesh, hoping that she wasn't being viewed on a bank of monitors somewhere. When she climbed between the cool sheets she had enough energy to jump up and run a marathon.

He kissed me.

And tomorrow…

This whole situation had gotten completely out of

control and she couldn't help being scared of how things would end up, but for now she just wanted to enjoy the ride.

She averted her eyes while Darias toweled off his well-muscled body, not wanting to alarm the heat sensors. She held her breath while he lifted the sheets and got into bed with her. Her stomach tightened as he leaned toward her and kissed her very gently on the lips.

Had he changed his mind? Her insides flashed to life in anticipation.

But he pulled back, eyes shining in the dark. "Good night. Or it would be if I could be sure we were really alone." He glanced around the dark corners of the room. Then he leaned in again and whispered. "But tomorrow we'll make up for lost time."

When Emma woke in the morning, Darias was gone. She realized she'd overslept, and it was nearly nine. Not surprising because she'd been far too overstimulated to fall asleep, even after how late they'd finally gone to bed.

She contemplated texting him to say she was looking forward to their encounter, then realized that would have been the first time ever that she'd sent him a purely personal text—he should probably take the lead in that under the circumstances—and besides, depending on where he was, someone else might see it.

She dressed and headed downstairs, wondering if she'd missed breakfast, but when she got there it was in full swing and everyone was dressed even more elegantly than usual.

"Ah, Emma, my dear." Darias's mom rushed toward her. "You must come meet my sister. Liesel has just arrived this morning from Bavaria." She took Emma's hand and led her toward one end of the long dining room table, where an elegant blonde woman, not as pretty as Carolina but close, was holding court with some of Darias's siblings while eating a grapefruit with a spoon. They were unwrapping and eating what looked to be handmade chocolates that she'd brought, which was funny since they were all in their twenties, not in elementary school. Maybe the chocolates were that good.

"This is Darias's new wife, Emma."

Emma shoved out her hand. Liesel looked up and studied Emma's face. A flicker of curiosity—or was it distaste?—crossed her fine features. Emma drew her hand back, since Liesel made no move to shake it. "Pleased to meet you," she fibbed. Royal etiquette was part of her "job."

Liesel ignored her greeting and instead studied her slowly from head to toe with pale blue eyes. "You're American."

"Yes. I'm from New Jersey." She tried to sound cheerful about it, though she felt more intimidated every second. She searched her mind for further conversation, then realized it might not be her place to babble on to this strange woman she knew little about.

"Isn't she lovely?" Darias's mom, Carolina, gestured to her as if she were a painting, not a person.

Which in fact, she now was, not that any of them knew yet.

"Very tall." Liesel peered up at her as if she were six feet tall. "But then I suppose that suits your lanky son."

"Darias's not lanky. You saw him this morning."

Liesel shrugged and bit into a crisp toast triangle. "That boy was a beanpole even as a toddler. He has grown into a handsome man, though, and seems reasonably intelligent."

Emma stared at Carolina. Was she going to let her sister talk like this about her own son, soon to be the king of this country?

"You're not royal though, are you?" Liesel turned her chilly gaze back to Emma. "Or even from the aristocracy."

"America doesn't have an aristocracy. Unless you count the Kennedys. And they're all cursed." Uh-oh, she was babbling. And possibly being offensive. But it was hard to keep still and smile with this much hostility being directed at you. "Everyone's been so generous in welcoming me into the family and helping me feel at home here." She hoped she didn't sound too reproachful. Where was Beatriz? She wasn't sure whether Beatriz and Liesel would be bosom buddies or archenemies.

"How marvelous," said Liesel, drily. She spoke perfect English with only the faintest accent. "I'm still amazed you're all carrying on like there isn't a murderer in your midst."

"It's what Emil would have wanted," protested Darias's mom. "He said that as a member of the royal family it's our duty to keep going no matter what."

"I don't think he had a vision of his naked corpse

on the floor when he said that."

"Liesel!" Carolina hissed and glanced around. "I told you that in confidence."

"Dad was found naked?" Rigo, one of the older brothers, stared at her. "How?"

"It's not important for you to know that. Liesel, really! These are his children."

"Surely it's important for everyone to know the facts." Her sister sipped her coffee. "One can face the truth bravely without hiding from it."

"I don't want word to get out. Emil wouldn't have wanted that. And don't say anything about what happened to Sofia, either."

"What about Grandma, Mama?" Cosima, a younger daughter, spoke up. "Why are you being so mysterious? We're all adults. We have a right to know."

Carolina's eyes filled with tears. "It's just so...so..." She rose from her chair and ran from the room. Emma found herself on her feet, wanting to run after her and comfort her, but several others did the same thing.

"Be gentle with her, Aunt Liesel," scolded Sandro gently. "She's feeling very raw. Her grief is terrible."

"I think the circumstances are very suspicious, that's all." Liesel lifted a thin brow. "I think something underhanded was going on and I think the details should be made public so that the investigation can progress. I don't like this cloak-and-dagger business."

"Our mother is very anxious to preserve the family's reputation." Sandro stood, towering over Liesel. "As well she should, since she is its head until Darias is crowned tomorrow."

"Where is that young firebrand? Probably off painting in his attic. I heard he caused a stir assaulting a security guard in the dead of night after a painting session. You think he'd be taking his life more seriously now he has royal duties."

"I was painting at three in the morning because that is the one time I don't have any royal duties." Darias's voice boomed from behind them, and they all turned around.

"I hear your lovely wife was with you." Liesel cast a dismissive glance at Emma.

"I cherish every second that I spend with my beautiful wife." Darias came up behind her and kissed her softly on the cheek. Her eyes slid shut as she enjoyed the warmth of his lips. No need to pretend she enjoyed the gesture; it made her heart flutter like a leaf.

"I'm sure you do." Liesel studied him. "I can't believe you kept her hidden from the family until now."

"You know I don't enjoy publicity for its own sake."

Liesel cocked her head. "Was it love at first sight?" She looked right at Emma.

Whose adrenaline spiked. "Absolutely," she blurted. "Though I didn't realize it at the time."

"Did you know he was a prince?"

"I had no idea who he was," she said honestly. "I just thought he was very handsome."

"Indeed he is. Let's just hope he's more sensible than his father."

"What?" Carolina, who'd been brought back into the room, looked shocked. "Whatever do you

JENNIFER LEWIS

mean, Liesel?"

"I mean to get himself murdered…under such bizarre circumstances. One must be very careful when one is royal."

"We've never had anything like this happen before in Altaleone. We have the lowest crime rate in continental Europe. Possibly anywhere in the world. It's an aberration."

"And still unsolved. What are you doing about the murders, Darias?"

Emma shivered. She'd already developed a deep dislike of Carolina's sister, who seemed to be poking wounds for no reason other than her own pleasure. Hopefully, she would leave soon after the coronation.

"I am conducting a private investigation, alongside the official one. I will not be disclosing any details. Your discretion in all matters related to our family is both requested and required."

Emma's heart warmed at his stern tone. He clearly didn't like his aunt any more than she did.

Liesel lifted her chin. "Such a commanding young man. Excellent king material."

Darias gave her a withering look. "I have business to attend to. My wife will accompany me." He held his arm out to Emma, who took it with relief, even though she hadn't managed a bite of breakfast yet. Anything to get away from his toxic aunt.

They exited the palace through the front door, down the wide flight of steps into the elegant courtyard. "Thank you for saving me." She wasn't sure if she should be blunt about one of his relatives.

"That woman is a menace. I'm sure she has some kind of agenda. I just haven't figured out what it is yet."

"I hope she doesn't upset your mom too much."

"My mom puts up with her bullshit because they're sisters. She's all about unconditional love."

"Your mom is one of the nicest, warmest people I've ever met."

"I told you that before you met her." Darias smiled. "But that makes her vulnerable to manipulative schemers. She can't see through them the way you and I can."

Emma wasn't so sure she could, either. "Hopefully, she'll leave soon after the coronation."

"I intend to make sure of it, one way or another. Meanwhile, I've been thinking that we should move into the old castle, so my mom can stay in the palace where she has so many memories without us all being on top of each other."

"We're hardly on top of each other in a palace with over a hundred rooms."

"True." Darias nodded to the guard as they walked out through the wrought iron gates between the palace and the village of Casteleone. "But we'll have more privacy and won't have to put on a show of any kind."

Emma felt a twinge of sadness. She'd hoped they wouldn't have to put on a show because their fake marriage was growing into a real one. Clearly, Darias's thoughts weren't heading in the same direction."

"I suppose you're right. Your grandmother the queen lived there, didn't she?"

"Yes, so it's all reasonably up to date, though a woman in her late seventies obviously has somewhat different tastes than we do." He grinned. "But we can make changes."

She liked the way he was saying "we," as though her opinions really mattered.

Even though she would be here for only one year.

"Do you want to go look at it now?" She noticed their feet were heading in that vague direction over the cobbled streets. Hanging baskets filled with white flowers for the wedding were being refilled with more colorful mixes—blue and gold, and burgundy and gold—for the coronation the next day. Workers and people in the street nodded and smiled respectfully as they walked by.

"Yes." Darias leaned in to speak lower. "I also think it will be easier to secure and control our privacy. It's a lot smaller than the palace and completely surrounded by a wall and a moat. I don't like the idea of cameras and sensors and spying eyes everywhere. It's compact enough that all staff can live in the village, and we can enjoy complete privacy."

"Would you mind if we stopped at a pastry shop? I came down just before you did and didn't eat breakfast yet." She didn't have any money on her. In fact, she'd stopped carrying it. Money seemed strangely useless when you had everything handed to you on a silver platter. "If you have any money. I'm afraid I don't." Maybe he didn't need it. Perhaps everything just arrived on a silver platter when you were royal.

"Of course. We'll stop at my favorite patisserie." Darias accompanied her into a quaint little shop, shelves piled high with shiny pastries and frothy cakes. They chose a selection of delicacies, then sat outside at a tiny wrought iron table while an aproned waiter brought them tiny steaming coffees.

"This is heaven, Darias. Altaleone is like a little charmed paradise. I find it strange that you prefer to live in New York."

"It's a very tiny paradise, where everyone watches my every move closely. I've enjoyed the anonymity and freedom of New York more than I like to admit. I'm ready to embrace my destiny, though." He spoke low, obviously not wanting strangers to overhear, and his warm breath grazed her skin, sending a ripple of pleasure through her.

She wanted to kiss him but knew that was inappropriate here on a public street, even if there were no pedestrians walking by at that exact second.

Then he leaned in very close and whispered. "But right now, the only paradise I crave is one where I can make love to you away from curious gossips and spying eyes."

14

"Is the old castle in the village private enough?" She spoke as quietly as possible. Maybe that was where they were headed.

Darias shook his head. "It's still something of a crime scene, even though the murders didn't happen there. Gibran's team is going through my grandmother's papers and effects, looking for clues."

"Have they found any?"

"Nope." He sipped his coffee. "No weird sex toys or kinky outfits. No revealing diaries. Only the correspondence and wardrobe of a busy monarch with a passion for her rose garden."

"You're sure she didn't have some kind of secret lifestyle." It wasn't a question, more of a statement. She knew Darias was horrified by the idea. But she couldn't help wondering if he was being blind because this was his sweet old grandma.

"Absolutely sure. And my father, too. He was no angel, mind you. I'm pretty sure he had affairs over the years. In fact, there may even be a longtime mistress somewhere, mourning him. I have no proof, though. You don't realize how little you really know someone until they vanish out of your life under mysterious circumstances." His jaw set in a hard line, and he put his cup down with a clatter. "But I'm gathering information. Sooner or later the broken pieces will join together and form a picture."

She ate an apricot tart carefully. Tiny pieces of pastry stuck to her lips, and the sticky apricot jam got on her fingers. Darias watched her tongue at work, and his face softened. "Thank goodness you are here to keep me sane. To be my muse."

His muse? He was painting her. She felt quietly honored. "How long does it take you to make a painting?"

"Depends. Sometimes months, sometimes just a week. Sometimes it depends on how long I want to stare at my model." His gaze hovered over her mouth, making her lips swell and part. "With you...I might have to do a whole series."

She smiled. "I'd like that."

"You didn't find it hard to sit still?"

"Not at all. Besides, he doesn't mind if I move." It was very easy to sit there and watch Darias at work. Finally she had an excuse to just stare at him. "It's relaxing. I feel important without actually doing anything."

Darias laughed. "Then you know what it feels like to be royal. People stare at you, they're curious and envious and admiring, and you didn't do anything except get up in the morning. It used to really annoy me."

"And now?"

"I'm just used to it, I guess. Has its benefits. I had a much easier time finding gallery representation than most artists, for example."

"But Keane Moss wouldn't have taken you on if you were drawing stick figures in pencil."

"Wouldn't he?" Darias stirred his coffee. "Maybe I'm more cynical than you. You'd be surprised by how excited people get about hanging with royalty, even royalty from a tiny country like Altaleone."

"It must be weird never knowing if people like you for yourself or because you're a prince."

"It makes you cherish opportunities to meet strangers who know nothing about you." His eyes twinkled.

"Like me. But once you introduce yourself it's all ruined. Unless you give a fake name and pretend you're someone else. Have you ever done that?"

"Once or twice." A wry smile tugged at his mouth. "When I was much younger. After a while I grew confident that people appreciated me for who I really am."

"I appreciate you." She could admit that. Especially if she intended to make love to him, which was apparently still on the agenda. Sexual energy wafted in the air between them like the steam from their coffees. She wanted to touch him desperately.

Would it be so wrong? They were married after all.

She liked him. He liked her.

"Where can we go for some privacy?" Was she being too pushy? The suspense was killing her.

A smile creased Darias's face. "I'm shocked. It's still morning."

She bit her lip. All these nights lying next to him

had done something to her mind and body. And of course it had been a *very* long time since she'd enjoyed any kind of sex, so her hormones were bubbling over.

"Sorry to shock you."

"I love it." He placed his hand over hers, and the heat from his palm sent a wave of excitement through her. "Let's go."

She wiped crumbs from her fingers, rose, and Darias held out his arm for her. She took it, and they were a few steps away from the restaurant when she remembered. "Do royals not have to pay for anything?"

"Not with our pennies." He lifted a brow. "Everyone in the world knows where we live so they can just send a bill to our house."

"I guess they know you're good for it."

"That, too. My family's been eating pastries at that shop since the mid-eighteenth century. Still owned by the same family, too."

"It must be very grounding living surrounded by so much history."

"*Oppressive* is one word." He chuckled. "But I'm learning to embrace that, too." He leaned in close enough to bump her gently as they walked. "And you're about to learn one of my little secrets."

"What?" A tiny prickly of anticipation—or was it nerves?—spiked deep inside her.

He didn't answer but simply led her along the picturesque cobbled street. They turned into a tiny side street. He pulled car keys from his pocket and pressed a button on the remote, and an ancient-looking double door opened to reveal a shiny black sports car. "My undercover disguise."

She grinned. "Oh, yes. I'm sure *no one* knows it's you. What is it, a Lamborghini?"

"Ferrari. Much more low-key. You'd be surprised by how many black Ferraris there are in Altaleone."

"I'm sure I would." They climbed in, which involved almost lying on the floor because the seats were angled back. Darias backed out expertly in the tight space, and they headed through the town and out toward the fields around it.

This time they went in the opposite direction of the summer palace, where the murders happened. They started out climbing through similar daisy-strewn fields with herds of placid cows and sheep, but as the climb grew steeper, the landscape became more forbidding and treeless. Soon there were no animals or buildings, and the road had narrowed to a one-lane track.

"Where are we going?"

"The desolate valley. That's what it's called in our language."

"Sounds lovely," she teased.

"It's very lonely. Which is exactly what I'm looking for right now."

"You want to write some soulful poetry."

"Yes." He turned and flashed her a dark glance. "With my tongue. On your body."

Her body responded with a shimmer of arousal. But there was nothing around them but jagged rocks and the beginning of what looked like a long, deep lake. "That sounds intriguing. But this landscape looks like the background in the *Mona*

Lisa. Are we going to perch on a rock?"

He smiled. "I have another secret."

A secret royal sex shack in the mountains? Nothing would surprise her at this point. They followed the shore of the dark lake, then climbed even higher, past some of the sharpest peaks she'd seen. She even glimpsed a mountain goat on one near-vertical surface. Then the rocks parted and they drove into a smooth green oasis, ringed by rocks, with a mossy carpet specked with tiny white flowers.

"Wow." She looked around her as he stopped the car. "Is this a volcano crater?" She climbed out of the car and studied their surroundings. The rocks formed a perfect circle.

"Yes. It's been extinct for a very long time. The rich soil grows this soft grass." He helped her from the car. "But even shepherds don't bother to come all the way up here anymore. Most people in Casteleone probably think it's just a legend.

"Stunning." She reached down and touched the mix of grass and moss that felt like silky carpet. The sky above was a bright sapphire blue that only added to the otherworldly atmosphere. "I feel like we're the last people left on earth."

"Let's pretend we are." He took her in his arms and pulled her close until her chest bumped against his. She drank in the warm male scent of him. When his lips met hers, her eyes closed and emotion swelled in her heart.

She'd learned so much about Darias in the past couple of weeks. In addition to being confident and commanding, he was warm and funny and cared deeply about the people who were important to him—which to a certain extent was everyone in Altaleone. Darias was truly a prince among men, royal titles aside. She'd never met anyone like him.

His fingers slid inside the waistband of her fitted pants and reached for the lace top of her panties, but the pants were too tight for his hand to slide in. His fingers roamed around to the front and undid them, then he resumed journey, caressing her backside, kissing her all the while.

Her hands followed the hollow of his spine down to his firm butt and slid inside his black jeans with ease. She felt his arousal harden against her belly, and their kiss deepened. His tongue probed her mouth, and she felt a tiny moan of pleasure rise from deep inside her. Already she was so aroused she might explode.

Were they really going to rip their clothes off right here up on this mountain top? She was ready to tear his off with her teeth. She fumbled with the buttons of his shirt, managing to undo them, then undid his jeans and pulled his shirt loose.

As he lifted her top over her head, her eyes opened for a moment and she looked right into his—which were dark with lust. "What if a plane flies over?"

"What if a butterfly flies over?" he taunted her, mischief playing around his mouth. "That's much more likely."

"I don't think I'd notice."

"I intend to make sure of it." Clothes half off already, he reached into the vestigial trunk of his Ferrari and pulled out a soft gray blanket, then spread it on the ground with a flourish. "Come here."

She stepped into his embrace, then he sank slowly down in front of her, pleasuring her with his tongue. Her neck, then her nipples. Then he traced a tantalizing wavy line down over her belly to her crotch. She let out the strangest little sigh as his tongue pushed into her private places, hot and cold at the same time.

She clutched at his hair while he licked her, making her buck with pleasure. She'd just started to get worried that her knees would give way and that she'd crumple in a heap on top of him, when he rose up again and lowered them both gently to the blanket.

He rolled on a condom and climbed over her. She shivered slightly, despite the warm summer air, her body wound so tight with pent up desire that she could barely contain it. He eased himself down until his erection brushed her belly, which was so sensitive that she gasped audibly.

He kissed her softly as he entered her. She felt herself open for him, so aroused that there was no resistance. He filled her and she kissed him back, all her foolish hopes and fears mingling into intense passion.

She'd never met anyone like Darias—so confident, capable and ridiculously gorgeous. He'd swept into her life like a tornado and blown it apart.

Now, in his arms she felt whole again, filled with joy and excitement. The way he moved inside her sent shockwaves of pleasure rippling to her toes. She wriggled under him, enjoying each new sensation that drew her deeper into a state of bliss.

Her hips rose to meet his as he quickened the rhythm, brushing her face with kisses and nuzzling into her hair. The tenderness of his kisses touched her heart. Could this really be the beginning of a true partnership between them?

The rhythm grew more insistent and she heard a rumble rise in his chest. Tension built inside her, growing and swelling and sweeping through her body until she couldn't hold it back any longer, and her climax exploded through her. Darias let out a low groan and she felt him shudder, then his arms tightened around her and they fell to the blanket together.

They lay there, gasping and holding each other for what felt like a long time—and a very short one. Gradually Emma opened her eyes, almost surprised by the bright sun and the clear blue canopy overhead. She turned to look at Darias and saw his eyes crack open just a little.

"You have no idea how much I've been wanting to do that." His voice was so low it was almost a rasp.

"Me, too," she admitted. "We'd agreed not to, so I tried to keep my feelings to myself."

"I don't think I ever really imagined I'd be able to live with you for a year without making love to you." He leaned in and kissed her softly on the lips again. "You're far too lovely for that."

Her chest tightened. So he'd known all along that they'd end up kissing? Maybe he'd known that even when they signed the contract. Maybe he'd made his negotiations with her—a strictly business arrangement—knowing full well that he'd get to enjoy some funny business on the side. Of course, when you were a gorgeous, wealthy prince—soon to be king of your own nation— you could probably anticipate getting whatever you want, whenever you want it.

"What's the matter?" He stroked her cheek.

"I really thought this was a business arrangement," she admitted. "When I agreed to it."

A cheeky smile creased his face. "Business is always better when mixed with pleasure."

"So our agreement is still in force?" She tried to keep her voice from shaking. *One year. Just one year.*

"Of course." He smiled. Clearly, he found nothing disturbing about that. "I pledged to uphold my side of the agreement, and I am a man of my word."

Maybe he thought she was worried he'd try to avoid paying her now that they'd become intimate. She didn't think that for a minute. In many ways, she trusted Darias completely.

Just not with her heart.

"I suppose we should put our clothes back on. We're scandalizing the butterflies." She tried to sound breezy. She really should just live in the moment and enjoy this delicious intimacy with such a gorgeous and wonderful man.

He deserved to enjoy it, too. He was under a lot of pressure, trying to get up to speed to rule a country and meet the expectations of family and strangers alike. She didn't want to add to his burden by asking too many questions or making inappropriate demands.

You knew what you were getting into. It's your fault if you're letting your feelings get involved.

Darias had rolled to one side, still holding her close in his arms. "The butterflies will keep our secrets. Not that we really have any. How is it wrong for two married people to make love?"

"It isn't. In fact, it would be weird if we didn't. You probably should have written it into the contract." She was joking, trying to make light of the situation.

"Would you have signed it if I had?" He lifted an eyebrow slightly.

"No." That would have made her feel like a prostitute. This whole situation was so strange and messy. If she'd had any idea what she was really getting into....

What would she have done? Right now, she really didn't know.

"So it's lucky I didn't."

"I suppose so." She kissed him back, not wanting him to sense all the doubts and fears roiling her brain. "I'd be in New Jersey, writing lesson plans, and you'd have had to find someone else to marry."

He chuckled and buried his face in her hair. "Perish the thought."

"I wonder who it would have been? Maybe the other gallery assistant, Farah. She's taller than me and twice as pretty."

Darias laughed. "She's nothing like as beautiful as you. I can't imagine any other woman as my queen."

For a year.

She didn't add that last part. He'd hired her

because he didn't want a real, permanent queen. His freedom was more important.

"You're sweet. And so far I'm enjoying this adventure. Who'd ever think that a girl from South Orange would get to live in a royal palace? It sounds like something you'd read about in the tabloids."

"I'm sure people *are* reading about it in the tabloids." He sounded rueful. "Luckily, we don't get them here in Altaleone. Though I suppose I should run a check to make sure the strange details of the murders haven't leaked. I don't want anyone surprising my mom with awkward questions at the coronation tomorrow."

"Do you think they would?"

"Reporters would love to. Maybe even jealous acquaintances. Royals always have a lot of haters," he said with a grin. "Goes with the territory."

"If the person who did the murders wanted scandal, then sooner or later they'll spread the story themselves."

"In a way I'd welcome that, then we could find them." He sighed and held her close.

A bird circled over them, so high in the sky she couldn't make out what kind it was. A hawk or kestrel or a vulture. She pointed to it. "A spy."

"They're everywhere these days. I suppose that's our cue to return to civilization."

"Tomorrow you'll be king."

"I will, whether my enemies want it or not."

"Are you afraid?"

"Never."

15

That night they made love in a tense and sexy silence, then slept holding each other. Emma alternated between sensations of deep bliss and fear of where this would end up. She told herself to live in the present.

In the morning they rose bright and early for the coronation. It would have been hard not to, for the town of Altaleone bustled with preparations—bands tuning, servants rushing around carrying trays of glasses and bottles of champagne, guests arriving by plane, train and car, villagers already lining the streets, jostling for the best place to see the royal procession.

Darias vanished early on to join his ministers in preparing for the ceremony, and Emma was left alone with the family as usual. Beatriz had helped her choose a dress to wear, and for the first time she also wore a jaunty hat in a matching jade green that made her feel both ridiculous and royal at the same time.

The coronation would take place in the town's ancient cathedral, and the royals headed there early to wait for Darias to arrive with his ministers in a state procession. Emma could feel eyes on her as they emerged from a fleet of limos in front of the church, and walked down the aisle toward the altar. Seated in the front pews between Beatriz and Darias's brother Rigo, Emma distracted herself by looking at the printed program—none of which was in English—and the elaborate carvings and paintings of the beautiful old church. Television cameras were set up on tripods inside the church, and Emma knew she had to keep a half-smiling poker face on at all times. She was managing fine until she heard a whisper in her ear and recognized Liesel's voice. "People are shocked that Darias has married a commoner. It's the first time in Altaleone history."

Emma didn't want to reply but also couldn't risk being rude in public. "I'm lucky he's open-minded."

"Far too open-minded, in my opinion. And I heard he is painting again. A king should not waste his time on idle pursuits."

"Surely even a king deserves some time to enjoy a hobby." She knew Darias would hate her calling his art a hobby—especially when he earned a fortune for each piece—but she was humoring Liesel.

"A king should pursue traditional activities like hunting and horse riding. It's your duty as his...wife...to shape his interests." The way she said *wife* made it sound like an insult. "But then you're not a real wife, are you?"

Emma's blood ran cold. Liesel's whisper was barely audible even with her coral-painted lips practically glued to Emma's ear. She didn't want to draw attention from either the gathered audience of domestic and foreign dignitaries, or the other family members, so she turned and whispered—rather louder—"I'm afraid I can't hear you over the organ music." She pushed a bright smile to her lips.

Liesel lifted a brow. Her sister, Carolina, sitting next to her, glanced from Emma to Liesel. "What's going on?"

"I was just telling Emma…" Liesel stared so hard at Emma that her heart began to pound. "About the importance of royal tradition. Being of common background, she has a lot to learn."

"She's right, of course," managed Emma with another smile, this time directed at Carolina. She really did like Darias's mom, who'd been nothing but warm and welcoming to her. "I'm doing my best to learn fast so I don't embarrass you all."

"You could never do that," said Carolina with a pat on her shoulder. "We're all thrilled to have you here."

"Are we?" Liesel murmured, half under her breath. Her words were hidden under Emma's "thank you" to her much nicer sister, but Emma still heard them. Probably some of Darias's siblings did, too, though no one said anything. They weren't supposed to be talking at all. The booming organ cast an atmosphere of ceremonial formality over the Baroque church nave, with its big frescoes of prophets and angels suspended over their heads.

Emma turned back around, anxious to kill this uncomfortable conversation. If they could get through today without Darias being assassinated, she'd consider it a success. She couldn't let herself get distracted by a bitter relative with some unknown axe to grind.

At last the organ music boomed louder, and she turned—along with everyone in the church—to see Darias entering, dressed in a ceremonial uniform even more ornate than the one he'd worn at their wedding. Flanked by ministers in red coats and funny old-fashioned hats, he walked down the center aisle toward the altar, where more men in colorful clothing from former centuries gathered, bearing a golden cup, a long gold sword and a very ornate crown.

Darias wore a grim and regal expression as he strode over the inlaid marble floor. Bare headed and insanely gorgeous, he was undoubtedly the most handsome man ever to have been crowned king. The fact that she was married to him just made the situation all the more ridiculous, and Emma felt herself stifling hysterical laughter.

It's just nerves! She dug her nails into her palms to calm herself. This was probably the most solemn and momentous moment of Darias's whole life. He was taking on a heavy mantle of responsibility and doing it with a grace and dignity that anyone could admire.

Turned to watch him, she found herself scanning the gathered audience, eyes peeled for anyone with questionable intentions. Dressed in their ceremonial uniforms or frumpy hats, the guests were as poker faced as herself and gave away nothing.

They all watched in silence as he ascended the steps to the altar. As he turned to face the crowd, his eyes met hers and held her gaze for a burning second. She couldn't breathe. The moment held so much meaning. For that instant she felt like his real wife, his partner who meant the world to him. He sat on the throne and the ceremony commenced, with a lot of mumbling in the local dialect that sounded like Italian—but wasn't quite—and he was tapped on the head with the sword and given a swallow from the big bejeweled cup and finally the crown was placed on his head.

The whole ceremony was so silent and loaded that Emma hoped there'd be a big cheer or something to release tension. No such luck. Darias rose and began to speak a long piece in his native language. She'd been trying to learn it, but there was no handy digital course, just books, and it was hard to study the pronunciation so she'd made little progress. She felt like a boob, sitting there among people who understood what he was saying.

She consoled herself with the thought that Liesel, who spoke German and had never lived in Altaleone, probably didn't understand more than the odd word, either.

At long last Darias headed back down the steps and toward her. He took her hand—the thrill of awareness swept right through her—and led her back through the church at his side. The moment was so loaded and emotional it was all she could do not to cry. It helped to remind herself that none of this was real, not for her. It was a job and she had a role to play, so she'd darn well better play it right.

Darias helped her up into the ceremonial carriage, led by four horses, and climbed in next to her.

The crowd roared as the carriage started moving along the cobbled street, bouncing a little on the stones.

"I missed you." He spoke low, while waving to the crowds.

"I missed you, too." She kept her public smile on her face.

"I can't wait to get you alone." His words crept into her ears, while he continued looking and waving at the crowds.

"Good luck with that," she said, teasing. "I have a feeling it's going to be—"

She didn't finish her sentence because at that moment a man exploded from the crowd, ran in front of the horses and hurled a lit firecracker.

Emma screamed as the horses leaped in all directions—or attempted to, but found themselves bound by harness and the carriage behind them. They skittered sideways, and the carriage tilted, throwing her into Darias's arms before the carriage overturned and they were flung hard onto the cobbled sidewalk and the rapidly scattering crowd.

Darias's body broke her fall, and he wrapped his arms around her, protecting her. The horses screamed, dragging the overturned carriage, as the footmen, who had jumped to the ground, struggled to get them under control.

"Are you okay?" She'd come down on him very hard.

"Yes." He helped her to her feet. "And you?" He scanned her quickly.

"I'm fine. No thanks to that crazy— Who did it?" She hadn't taken a good look at the man with the firework, and she couldn't see past the chaos of the carriage.

Darias squeezed her hand. "We'll find him. He can't have gone far in this crowd."

Staff had rushed in to fuss over Darias and her, and he brushed them away. "Is the assailant in custody?"

"Yes, your majesty." Emma heard the word *majesty* and sighed with relief that at least the coronation hadn't been interrupted. "He appears to be a student."

"Bring him to me."

"Uh…" The guard hesitated. "Our men have him in custody. He'll be taken to the police station."

"I want to lay eyes on him." Darias took her hand and led her along with him.

The horses were back under control but still dancing nervously in place as their attendants unharnessed them from the wrecked carriage. Darias patted the neck of the nearest one as they passed.

The guards attempted to dissuade Darias from confronting the man, but Darias continued to insist—in his language—until they brought him to a police van and rolled down the window. From where she stood, Emma could see a dark-haired young man wedged between two uniformed policemen.

"Why did you throw the firework?" Darias spoke in English.

The captive replied in the local language, and once again Emma cursed her lack of understanding. Darias snorted with disgust. "You're lucky you didn't hurt one of my horses.

Deliberately injuring a horse is still a capital crime in Altaleone." He stared at the man for a moment. "Don't think I'm done with you." Then he spoke rapidly to the guards and moved back toward the main street.

"We can continue on foot," he suggested. "As long as your shoes aren't too uncomfortable."

"They're fine." She'd discovered recently that very expensive footwear was surprisingly comfortable, even when dangerously high. "Would you really kill someone for injuring a horse?" The idea was both horrifying and fascinating.

"It hasn't happened since 1899, but it's one of those laws that's good to keep on the books just to keep people on their toes." Humor flashed in his eyes, and she was glad to see it there instead of the blind rage some men might feel when their coronation procession was ruined by a kid with a firework.

"What did he say?"

"I can't really say it out loud." He waved and smiled at the crowd. "It wouldn't be appropriate under the circumstances. I'll tell you later."

She could barely hear him anyway over the roar of the enthusiastic and supportive crowd. She felt proud, marching beside someone so unflappable and clearly liked and admired by the gathered throng.

Back at the palace there was feasting and partying very similar to the wedding. Her main duties consisted of smiling and making small talk with anyone who spoke English.

Beatriz steered her around, and she was beginning to feel that Beatriz was keeping her away from anyone who might ask too many probing questions. Did Beatriz know more than she let on? Or was she just anxious to prevent embarrassment to the royal family from the commoner in their midst? It was hard to tell.

Darias disappeared almost immediately—without a word—and she assumed he wanted to find out more about the attack during the procession. She was nervous that the kid with a firework might just be the tip of some larger and more dangerous iceberg. "Did the security guards search everyone who came to the palace?" she whispered to Beatriz, during a quiet moment.

"Of course not." Beatriz looked amused. "We can hardly have heads of state and ministers patted down and frisked. Gibran does have a lot of security staff—men and women—dressed as guests and wandering among the crowd."

Emma glanced around. They were probably the young, good-looking ones. Many guests at the coronation were elderly and weighed down with diamonds or medals. "I suppose that's a relief. I can't wait until it's over."

Beatriz sipped her champagne. The level of liquid never went down, though. Emma realized she was just pretending to drink it but wanted to stay stone-cold sober.

"It's not over until the mock battle."

"Battle?" Her mind sprang back to the note she'd read. Battle brings the sound of thunder. "What battle?"

"It's a reenactment of some silly conflict in 1292, when some local hotshot decided to invade Altaleone with his private army during a young prince's coronation as king, and ended up with his head on a platter." Beatriz smiled. "It's tradition to reenact it. They're actually still using the same weapons from the thirteenth century."

Did Darias tell anyone about the note other than Gibran? It had turned his suspicions to someone.... What was the name? "Is there a guest here called Lorenzo Aldobrando?"

Beatriz looked startled. "Uh, I'm not sure. I suspect he was invited, but I hope he knows better than to come."

"Why?"

"His family is very ancient like ours, and we've had our ups and downs over the centuries, but in recent years there's been some bad blood over business and an ancient dispute over some land."

"So you haven't seen him?"

"I'm not even sure I'd recognize him. I haven't seen him in years."

Emma decided to text Darias her concerns about the "battle," though she noticed disapproving glances when she pulled out her phone. The crowd in this room probably still sent messages by uniformed men on horses.

He texted her back right away. **Aldobrando is here. He's being watched closely.**

The message was not reassuring. She wanted to ask about the young man in custody but knew it wasn't appropriate to keep tapping away at her phone while the party swirled around her. **Will you be back here soon?**

She hated to sound needy, but still...

As soon as I can be.

She sucked in a breath, hoping no one could tell

how nervous she felt. What if she never saw Darias again? With all these threats and potential enemies in their midst, anything could happen. At least she'd done all she could to warn him.

"You look pale," said Beatriz, frowning. "You should eat something."

"I can't." She glanced around. "My stomach is in turmoil. The incident with the firework." She tried to whisper without seeming too obvious. "I keep thinking everyone is a potential assassin."

"Welcome to being royal." Beatriz looked grim. "And having a target on your forehead."

"Do you really always live in fear?"

"Not of being murdered, but the press are always out hunting for a juicy story so we have to be on our guard."

"I bet you've never done anything that would shock the press." Beatriz seemed the most straitlaced person imaginable.

"Probably true! I am deplorably dull." Her smile didn't reach her eyes. "Let's go see how Mama is getting on."

Emma could see at first glance that Carolina had not been quite so careful with the champagne as Beatriz. Her cheeks had high spots of color, and her eyes were filled with emotion. "I remember your father's coronation like it was yesterday," she gushed to Beatriz as they approached. "He was so handsome in his uniform. I loved him so terribly much."

"Did you even really know him by then?" Beatriz grabbed a plate of tiny snacks from a waiter and shoved them under her mom's nose. "I thought it was pretty much an arranged marriage."

"It was love at first sight." Darias's mom waved her hand in front of her face. "Oh, I know things grew more prosaic as time went on and we were both so busy, but on that day my love for him was like madness. I'll never forget it."

Beatrice patted her arm. "No one wants you to forget it, Mama. Have something to eat."

Carolina clearly didn't want to eat any more than Emma, because she waved the plate away and wrapped her arms around Emma, who tried to hug her back despite their crisp, formal dresses. "I'm so glad Darias found you right when he needed you."

"Me, too," she said quite honestly. Then felt a stab of guilt when she remembered how crushed his mom would be when the year was up and she packed her bags and left. Still, now wasn't the time to worry about that. Darias's mom needed her to be cheerful and useful. "Tell me about the fake battle."

"Oh, it's so ridiculous. I swear it's just an excuse for all these men to get dressed up in armor and wave swords around."

"Better that they do it in a ceremony than in a real battle," said Beatriz with a lifted brow.

"They wear suits of armor? Like, the kind that covers your face?" Emma's gut flashed an ugly warning.

"Yes, of course. The suits are all kept in the royal armory. They've never been worn in a real battle, of course, but—"

Darias's mom continued, but Emma's mind was working furiously. What if someone concealed their identity inside one of the suits?

She didn't want to voice her fears in front of Carolina. She knew Darias didn't want his mom worried or upset for any reason. But if the murderer was here…and intended to participate in the battle—

She needed to see Darias, and now.

16

Emma excused herself as if going to the ladies' room and headed upstairs to the bedroom she shared with Darias. There at least she could call him in peace. She dialed as she headed up the stairs, and he picked up on the first ring. She glanced around—the hall downstairs was filled with glittering guests and there were three different staffers on the staircase alone.

"Where are you?" she asked.

"I've been at the armory, where the boy is being held. I'm heading back in a security car right now. He's not who he says he is at all. He claimed to be a radical student, but I recognize him. He's the son of a prominent Piedmont family. I know his older brother."

Emma hurried along the hallway, out of sight of the guests downstairs. "Why did he do it?"

"To get my attention. That's all he would say. Now his expensive lawyers are here and he's clammed right up."

She was so frustrated to be talking into a phone, especially after the drama of earlier. She wanted to see him. "Darias, I'm still nervous about this mock battle and Aldobrando. If everyone's face is covered, how do you know who is who?"

"Good point. I'll make sure to eyeball them all. I've asked Gibran to sic Beatriz on Aldobrando. You know what she's like. He won't have a spare moment to get up to no good."

Emma laughed. "She's really taken care of me."

"I know she means well."

"I miss you," she said softly. She felt odd confessing it, but of course it played right into the loving-husband-and-wife charade, if anyone was listening in.

"I'll be back soon. Meet me at the main door."

She hung up, with a tiny ache that he didn't say anything about missing her. Then she chastised herself. He was busy being made king today, not to mention trying not to be assassinated. She needed to get over herself, and fast!

Emma tucked her phone into her pocket and descended the stairs again, eyes on the door. Out of the corner of her eye she saw Beatriz, severe and elegant in navy, greeting a tall, rather handsome man with a suspicious expression. That must be him. He didn't look like a murderer, but they never did, did they?

Aldobrando wore a slim, dark suit, a stark contrast with the gaudy braid and uniforms of so many men at the palace. She couldn't hear what he was saying, but she saw Beatriz crack a reluctant smile. No doubt he was a charmer.

Lucky thing Beatriz was the last woman on earth to fall for some hustler's charms.

The front door flew open and Darias strode in, flanked by guards. She couldn't stop the grin that spread across her face and she rushed to him, too fast for royal dignity.

He kissed her on the cheek, and she let herself luxuriate in the warmth that radiated from his lips. Relief swept through her that he was back. "Can I help you with anything? I'd love to watch you get ready for the mock battle."

"I think it's perfectly appropriate for a queen to gird her husband's loins for battle," he said with a mischievous smile. "Let me lead the way."

They entered a very large bedroom where six suits of armor had been disassembled into their component parts. Four men were already half dressed in theirs, and two stood empty. One— elaborately carved in both silver and gold—was set apart from the others. Darias approached it with a smile.

"We like to kid ourselves that these are the original medieval suits of armor, but the reality is that our ancestors were a good six inches shorter than us. There's been a lot of very skilled metalwork done on these in the last century."

He unbuttoned and shrugged off his uniform jacket. Emma glanced around, surprised that he would undress in front of everyone. Maybe she expected them to start bowing and scraping now that he was king, but he just chatted with them in their language like he was one of the guys.

"This is Paulo Fortis, one of my oldest friends." The tall blond man nodded. "And this is Vincenzo Lotti, son of the chief of the armory." She nodded at a bearded man with red hair. "Arlo and Fritz are twins, nephews of my mother, who visited us every summer as children." Both handsome and boyish, they nodded their hellos.

"Where's that scoundrel Rigo? He'll be late for his own wedding. I'd have preferred Sandro, but he sprained his wrist playing squash last week."

"He's coming," said Paulo. "But who's wearing the last suit?"

"Dom Bartolo." Darias frowned. "But now that you mention it I haven't seen him today. Let me call him."

Darias dialed, waited, then left a message. "That's odd."

Emma's gut did that weird warning thing again. Was the last suit somehow reserved for a killer? "Perhaps one of the security guards could wear it," she suggested.

"Do you think I trust one of those strangers to wield a sharp sword above my head?" Darias lifted a brow. "I'll call Rigo and tell him to bring someone."

He made the call, then she helped him don the suit over his shirt and underwear. It fastened with leather straps, and she tried not to overreact each time her fingers brushed his skin.

She couldn't wait to be alone with him tonight. As long as they were both alive by then.

Rigo burst in, "Sorry I'm late, bro. Got chatting with an old friend I haven't seen in ages. And I brought him to stand in for Dom." He beckoned someone into the doorway.

Emma's blood froze as she recognized Lorenzo Aldobrando.

"I didn't realize you two were friends," said Darias slowly. He probably hadn't warned his brother that Lorenzo was a suspect.

"It's been a long time," said Lorenzo, entering the

room confidently. "I know our families haven't been close for a long time, but it's time to change that. What am I wearing for the festivities?"

Emma blinked as one of the twins pointed to the last suit of armor. She glanced at Darias, who was watching Lorenzo closely. What was he up to? First talking to Beatriz, then Rigo, and now.... She knew Darias didn't need warning that this was a potentially dangerous situation.

Rigo and Lorenzo donned the armor, and the chief of the armory showed up to explain the ritual. None of them had ever seen it before, including the chief himself. It took Emma a while to realize that it would be on horseback—a joust. It had last been performed at Darias's father's coronation more than thirty-five years earlier. Three men, including Darias, would ride from one end of the courtyard, Darias would tilt with their leader, then he would win and the crowd would cheer and—

"I'll be your opponent," offered Lorenzo.

"Will you be able to keep the ceremonial nature of the event in mind?" asked Darias, drily. "Or are you hoping to take control of Altaleone this afternoon?"

Lorenzo laughed, a rich, rather disconcerting sound. "I can contain my ambitions and sporting instincts enough to perform the duty."

"That is a relief." Darias didn't look worried. But then he didn't look relaxed, either. They were all speaking English, probably for her benefit. "I don't believe you've met my wife, Emma."

The way he said it, gruff and...proprietary, made something sizzle deep inside her

"My pleasure." Lorenzo bowed low, as if it were the fourteenth century, not the twenty-first. "I do hope you'll excuse my changing in front of you."

"No problem," she managed, glad she didn't have to shake his hand. She wondered if that piece of paper with the poem should be checked for his fingerprints. She decided to make sure they got some as a sample. "Would you like me to help you with your armor?" If he touched the shiny metal before donning gloves, they'd get a clean sample.

She felt Darias's stern and surprised gaze on her. "I'm sure he can manage by himself."

She wanted to laugh. Was he jealous? She wished she could let him know her intentions.

"As long as I can figure out which way everything goes." To her relief he handled each piece, putting them in order. Now all she had to do was secure them after he took them off.

In less than five minutes she was walking along the hallway to the courtyard in the company of six clanking knights in armor. None had put their helmets on, as apparently they were very hard to see out of, the eye slits being angled for a man high on horseback.

They went out a door she'd never been through before, into a rectangular stable yard where six horses stood waiting. They weren't the strapping draft horses she'd imagined, more like slender thoroughbred racehorses, each decked out in a fringed and embroidered costume of a different color.

A crowd had started to gather around the edges of the courtyard. "Is it going to happen here? This area seems awfully small for a joust."

"It's been the tilting yard since 1320." Darias looked at her with amusement in his eyes. "Who am I to say it's too small?"

"I see what you mean. It's hard to argue with seven hundred years of tradition."

"Story of my life." He said it with good humor and donned his helmet. He was unrecognizable in the ornate armor but somehow still had a commanding presence that made others turn to him for guidance. He mounted first, with assistance from costumed attendants, and the others followed suit, then took their places at each end of the courtyard.

Why does everything involve horses around here? Emma found her heart racing at the prospect of something happening to spook the horses again. The center of the courtyard was hard gravel, but strips around the edge were floored with smooth, ancient cobbles that would probably be slippery in an emergency. She couldn't wait until this was over.

Each rider was given a tall lance, painted to match their horse's costume. Darias brandished his easily, though it didn't look light and she could see one of the twins struggling to keep his at the right angle.

And she didn't take her eyes of Lorenzo Aldobrando. He looked at ease atop his horse, holding his lance. He even tipped up the lid on his visor and looked out at the crowd. Was he looking for someone? Surely he wouldn't try anything stupid in this crowded courtyard in front of so many spectators.

Trumpets played a fanfare and Darias and Lorenzo circled their horses, then headed across the courtyard at a slow canter, lances raised high.

Emma held her breath as their lances met. They passed and circled, then did it again. On the third time Aldobrando dropped his lance with a flourish—as if wanting to show everyone it was intentional—and he and his men dismounted their horses and gave them to Darias and his men. Darias's team them rode around the courtyard—on the slippery cobbles—one time, while their "captors" stood in the middle, clapping graciously.

The whole thing was beyond weird. Why would a family "enemy" offer to play the role of a conquered one? Had he planned it all along, or was it truly an accident?

At last Darias dismounted and she hurried to him and helped get his helmet off. "We need to put your opponents' armor aside," she whispered, leaning in. "To check it for fingerprints."

Darias surprised her by wrapping his armored arms around her waist and squeezing her so hard she almost dropped the helmet. Luckily, an attendant grabbed it. She hoped no one had overheard her.

"What would I do without you?" He kissed her mouth, sending shivered of excitement through her.

"Good question." None of this would be happening without her. Unless he'd managed to find another royal bride at a few days' notice. Which probably wouldn't have been all that hard, considering.

"I'll make sure of it. Now we just have to get through the dinner and I'll finally have you to myself again."

She looked around, wanting to make sure Lorenzo Aldobrando didn't slip away. Her blood chilled as she looked up and down the courtyard, where the crowd had moved in to cover the gravel and fuss over the horses. "Where is Aldobrando?"

Darias glanced around. "I'll text Gibran." He pulled out his phone and typed rapidly. "Where's my mom? We need to keep her busy. I don't want her getting upset. The last time she saw this it was my dad riding." Emma chastised herself for forgetting all about Carolina in the commotion. "There she is." Darias strode over to her, still in his armor, and kissed her on her cheek.

"You make a very gallant knight," she whispered. Emma could see she held emotion hovering just beneath the surface. "Your father would be so proud."

How odd to think that his father could never have seen this moment because this whole ceremony depended on his death. It must be so odd to grow up knowing that the events of your life would follow a certain progression—whether you wanted them to or not.

Unless you threw a wrench in the works—like a nonroyal bride you found behind a desk at your art gallery.

"Are you all right?" Beatriz materialized behind her mom.

"I'm fine." Emma choked back the strange giggles that had risen to her throat. "Just way too much excitement for me. I think I'm getting hysterical." She tried to make it sound like she was joking.

"I know the feeling." Beatriz looked sympathetic. "Especially so soon after the wedding."

"And moving to a new country and meeting a big new family." Carolina stroked her cheek. "You are doing magnificently. We all just have to keep our game faces on for a few more hours." Her lips quivered as she pushed them into a smile. "After that?" She shrugged.

Emma wanted to hug her but contented herself with smiling back. She didn't want to upset royal protocol if she could help it.

"Now that your brother has vanquished me, will you join me for a drink?" All heads spun to see Lorenzo Aldobrando—already dressed again in his dark suit and with his hair slicked back neatly—approaching Beatriz.

Even unflappable Beatriz looked startled.

And he would have had time and opportunity to remove his fingerprints from the armor.

"Of course, darling, go on." Carolina prodded her. "Don't mind me. I'll be fine."

Emma realized that Darias's mom knew nothing about their suspicions. She glanced at Darias in time to see his eyes narrow slightly.

Beatriz looked suspicious. "Of course," she said in a clipped tone. "Lead the way." Lorenzo gave her his arm and she rather hesitantly slipped hers inside, as if she were slipping it into a lion's open mouth.

Which maybe she was.

The ceremonies continued well into the night, with speeches, feasting and music. Darias stayed at her side nearly all evening, only stepping away for occasional conversations with old family friends, ministers or visiting dignitaries. The mood was festive. Everyone seemed excited about the future with their new king—and queen.

She kept her smile steady despite the occasional twinge of guilt when someone else exclaimed over what a lovely couple they were and how bright the future of Altaleone shone with them at its helm.

Finally, after most of the guests had drunk themselves into a stupor and staggered off to bed, Darias made his excuses. He wrapped his arm around her waist as they ascended the stairs, and even staff members smiled at what an adorable couple they were. She could almost believe her own PR as she gleefully anticipated a night in Darias's arms.

They headed for their room, only to be intercepted by sheepish staff members who told Darias that their effects had all been moved to a different room.

As the crowned and reigning king, Darias had been moved—against his will and express wishes—into the traditional royal bedchamber recently occupied by his mother and father. All of their effects had been transferred while they were at the party, and Emma found it chilling to see her clothes hanging in the closet.

The contract! She'd forgotten all about it in the frenzy of wedding preparation. It was still in her solo bedroom, which had been packed up without her knowledge and which was no doubt occupied tonight by one of the guests. She'd better focus on getting it back because if that got into the

wrong hands....
Right now she couldn't even imagine what would
happen.

17

"I'm sorry about this unexpected move," Darias said softly, once he'd closed the door behind them. "I suspect my mom was behind it. She has a will of iron under her soft exterior."

"I do find it weird that people are handling our possessions without our knowledge. Possibly even snooping through them." She wondered, not for the first time, if she should tell him about the contract but chickened out again. Besides, despite Darias's reassurances that it wasn't, the room might be bugged.

"I'm used to it, but it is annoying. I'm sorry." His adorably contrite expression stole her heart. Not that he hadn't stolen it already.

"No worries. I signed up for it." She grinned and tried to sound lighthearted. "I wonder where they put my phone charger. I ran out of battery some time during the ceremonies."

"Here, use mine." He pulled one from the nightstand drawer as if he'd put it there himself. "At least with years of experience I know where they'll put my stuff." He plugged in her phone and put it on a beautiful inlaid dresser.

The room was huge, even bigger than the one

they'd shared before. Most two-story houses in New Jersey would fit comfortably inside it. The furnishings were very elaborate, polished wood with gold inlay that was probably real gold and gorgeous oil paintings of animals on the walls— probably some ancestors' cherished pets.

Her phone started to make noises as messages arrived, but she ignored it because Darias wrapped his arms around her waist and started to kiss her. Her belly melted, and her knees grew weak as emotion crept over her. All the tension and anxiety and excitement of the day evaporated out of her like steam under the heat of his kiss.

"Thank you for being my queen," he whispered between kisses.

His queen. She was! At least for now. The conflicting feelings made her chest ache.

"You're welcome. I'm enjoying the experience." A strange thing to say, at least if they had been a real couple.

Darias undressed her slowly, tantalizing her skin with his lips and tongue. "I've been waiting all day and night to do this." She wrestled with the buttons on his uniform, fingers impatient. It was hard to concentrate when he blew softly into her ear, sparking a cascade of sensation.

He helped her get his clothes off, and they made hungry, impatient love. She forgot all about the strange bedroom and the contract and all the strangers she'd smiled at today, and lost herself in Darias's arms. Afterward she lay there, wishing the moment could go on and on. Lying with her head on his chest, she could imagine their relationship slowly evolving into a true marriage where they shared their thoughts and dreams and grew old together as equals.

Then she woke up.

Her phone, now charged, vibrated angrily on the dresser across the room. Reluctant, she climbed out of bed—where was her robe? She had no idea. She walked across the room naked and retrieved it. Darias was still asleep, relaxed and beautiful with a big muscular arm flung across the pillow above his head.

She unplugged the phone and hurried back to bed and under the covers. Fifty-three text messages? Ouch. And thirteen phone calls. She decided to start with the calls. The first was from Viola, a college friend, who chastised her for not inviting her to the wedding. For the first time she felt bad that she hadn't invited any of her friends.

If it had been a real wedding, she would have. But it wasn't. How could she have them travel halfway across the world and probably buy an expensive gift when this whole wedding was just a charade to allow Darias to become king?

The next message was from another friend, from high school this time, first congratulating her warmly, then reminding her that they'd always promised to be each other's maid of honor.

Really? That must have been at least eight years ago. Did people even use a matron of honor these days? The only friend of hers who'd actually got married had an informal ceremony in Central Park and encouraged nearby strangers to join in and throw organic confetti.

Another message was from her Aunt Sallie, who lived in Nevada and whom she hadn't seen in five years since Sallie hadn't been able to attend her mom's funeral due to a cruise she'd already booked. She was also mad about not being invited. Apparently, the wedding had been all over the news media and now everyone she'd ever met was mad at her.

She was ready to delete the next message unheard, but it turned out to be from The Fountains. Her blood pressure spiked when it began with "I don't wish to alarm you but..." and went on to explain that her brother had gone missing the previous evening.

Gone missing? Weren't residents under close observation? It was a facility filled with addicts, whose thoughts habitually revolved around how to score their next fix. She sat up, pulled the covers around her and called back. She realized on the third ring that it was probably about three A.M. in New York right now, but someone answered. "What happened to Jonas?"

She heard an inhale. "I'm afraid that he went missing sometime right after dinner. He said he was heading back to his room to get something, then the nurse noticed he was missing at night check."

"Did you call the police?"

There was a pause. "Uh, no. If he's involved in something illegal, he could be arrested and charged."

"Of course." How did her brother get tangled up in drugs? Especially when he'd grown up knowing that his dad died of an overdose. Anger flashed through her, followed closely by fear. It was The Fountains job to help him, but once he'd walked off the property they might feel no further responsibility. "Is anyone looking for him?"

"Of course. We have someone who specializes in finding patients who go AWOL, and he quietly interviews them while they're here to figure out where they would be mostly likely to go at a time like this. We usually find them within twenty-four hours."

"Great. That's great to hear. Is there anything I can do to help?" She felt powerless and frustrated that she was thousands of miles away. It was not like she could just get on a plane. She had a job to do here, and she couldn't have Darias's family find out that thanks to her there was now a junkie in the extended family.

"Don't worry too much. We'll keep you posted."

She hung up and noticed that Darias was now propped on one elbow watching her.

"Your brother left The Fountains?"

She nodded. "I'm scared. My dad OD'd when I was seven." She wanted to remind him that Jonas was her last living family member, but Darias might find that odd or rude, since she was now surrounded by his entire large family.

Except that they weren't really family when it was only for one year.

He stroked her arm. "They're the best of the best. They'll take find him."

"And every girl I ever said hello to is mad that I didn't invite her to my wedding." She made quotation marks in the air with her fingers as she said *wedding*. "It's weird that I can't tell them the truth." She hadn't really thought about how people she rarely saw would react. It truly hadn't occurred to her that they'd even find out. Obviously, she just wasn't that smart. "I guess I didn't realize how much press the wedding would get. Why are they only finding out about it now?"

"People don't really care that much about Altaleone. A lot of them have never heard of it. I suppose the media outlets went for a two-for-one combo package."

"And now I have fifty-three text messages that I'm afraid to read."

Darias laughed. "You'll soon learn not to give your number to anyone that you don't *really* like."

"They'll probably all feel smug when the press announces our breakup a year from now." She tried to sound chirpy. She realized as she said it that she was hoping Darias would protest and say that—

She didn't know exactly what she was hoping for, but Darias didn't say anything. He looked at the sheets. Then at a large oil painting of a brindle greyhound.

"At least the coronation went smoothly. After the firework incident, that is." She babbled, saying anything to fill the awkward silence she'd created.

"I need to go find out what they've learned about the kid who did it." Darias propelled himself from the bed, probably glad of an excuse to get away from her.

She needed to learn to be happy with what she had—right now. *Nothing lasts forever.* Even people entering real marriages would probably end up splitting up and shedding tears sooner or later. She should be glad that at least she knew how this romance would end.

Darias was a ladies' man. Yes, she might be his current "muse," but she wasn't the first and she wouldn't be the last. And she'd better not forget that again.

Darias tugged on some clothes smart enough to encounter whatever dignitaries had stayed overnight and headed downstairs. Emma's statement—about their impending breakup—had rattled him. He wasn't even sure why. Wasn't that exactly how he planned it?

Maybe it was all going too smoothly. He hadn't expected her to end up in his bed so quickly. Or maybe he had and was disconcerted that he'd been right.

"Good morning, darling!" His mom greeted him at the bottom of the stairs with a kiss.

"You're glowing."

"With happiness. Out of the ashes, you know? Now you need to get used to people calling you your majesty. Is Emma sleeping in?"

"No, she's up. Just responding to phone messages. I'm sure she'll be down soon. I'll catch breakfast later. I want to meet with Gibran and get a bead on what happened yesterday."

"Of course." He hated the shadow of worry that passed over his mom's beautiful face. "Do take care."

"I will." He dialed Gibran as he walked out to his car and a staffer opened the door for him. "Any news?"

"His lawyers are arguing that it was a youthful prank."

"He's not that much of a youth. At least college

age. Is he still in custody?"

"Yes, but only because this is a monarchy and he attacked the king. Your lawyers tell me that it would otherwise be a misdemeanor since no one was hurt."

"Property was damaged. I'm sure the carriage has some scrapes. And my wife was scared." Protective rage filled him at the thought that Emma could have been hurt.

"Can you charge him with treason?" Gibran's voice was grim. "That may be the best way to hold him."

"And scare the truth out of him. Treason carries the death penalty. Of course it hasn't been used in recent centuries. If the lawyers say it will work, then do it. I want to talk to him now."

"He's in the old cells at the armory. We thought it best to keep him away from the general jail population."

"Good. I'll be right there." It was probably quicker to walk, but he was already in the car, so he drove and parked on the street outside the monolithic stone armory that dated back to the late middle ages.

The prisoner was in a simple stone cell with a built-in bench, and he sat on the bench as if waiting for his coffee at Starbucks, glancing up with seeming disinterest as Darias approached.

"I know you. I know your father is president of the Lesset Bank Group and that your sister, Lana, just graduated from Harvard. I've skied with your brother, Werner. Our fathers hunted together. What were you doing?" He didn't really expect an answer. Gibran told them he hadn't spoken except to his lawyers.

"Delivering a message."

"Oh?" Darias tried not to look too interested.

"You've been invited to join the Cross of Blood."

"I have no interest in joining some ancient society with bizarre rituals." *That might be behind the murders of my father and grandmother.*

"I think you'll find that you can't not join."

"I think you'll find that you will soon be charged with high treason." Darias stared at him, unblinking. Why would the son of a wealthy noble risk imprisonment and death? Usually, the reasons for crime could be traced back to either money, or power.

"What is the main objective of the Cross of Blood?"

"Join it and you will find out." The young man looked relaxed and confident, as if he'd just been challenged to a game of backgammon, not threatened with execution.

"What's in it for me?" *Apart from possible death.*

"Your destiny."

Darias sneered and decided he'd heard enough. He turned and walked back past the armed guards. Unfortunately, it appeared he would indeed have to join the Cross of Blood.

18

Emma headed downstairs tentatively, not sure what would be expected of her this morning. There were still many guests at the palace so she wore a dress and spent time on makeup, hoping to look appropriately royal.

She still hadn't even read all her fifty-three text messages. She had read enough to glean that the *National Enquirer* had put her and Darias on the cover with the garish headline "Jersey Girl Nabs Euro King." So all her former coworkers, her best friend from elementary school and her mom's neighbors had all learned of her whereabouts at the supermarket checkout counter.

She hadn't dared try to find the article.

Of course Darias was nowhere to be found, and she had to negotiate her way through a crowd at the buffet breakfast. "Thank you! The ceremony was very moving, wasn't it?" The small talk exhausted her. She'd never really needed it in her life before and didn't have practice.

She finally managed to gather herself a plate of sautéed ham and eggs and little brioche things, and make her way to an empty table—there were at least twenty small tables set up for guests near the usual big one—when she heard Liesel's voice behind her. "Good morning, Queen Emma."

"Good morning," she replied evenly, barely looking up. She was starving, and the ham smelled amazing.

To her dismay, Liesel sat down opposite her. "A Jersey girl—what does this mean?" She lifted a penciled brow. Great. She'd read the article.

"I think it's a type of tomato. My mom grew them." She attempted a smile.

Liesel frowned. "Your father died of a drug overdose. How tragic."

Uh-oh. Just how much information was in the article? Her stomach shriveled with worry at the reminder that Jonas was still missing on the streets of New York. "Yes. I was very young. I missed him a lot." No need to mention that he'd never actually lived with them.

"And this brother of yours? Tell me about him." Liesel tented her hands and rested her chin on them.

Emma's heart sank. Now she did wish she'd read the article. She didn't really want to reveal any more than Liesel already knew. "He's young. What have you heard about him?"

Liesel pursed her peach colored lips. "That he was swept into some kind of drug rehab place the moment Darias proposed to you. He's a drug user like his father."

Emma listened. Wondering how to respond. Did she know Jonas had left The Fountains? "He's been under a lot of pressure lately. Our mom died of cancer."

"So I read. The Leone family has never previously found itself the subject of the *National Enquirer*."

Emma's heart sank at the thought of how happy

Liesel would be on the day that the end of her marriage to Darias was announced. She could already hear that pinched mouth uttering the immortal words "I told you so."

"I haven't read the article." She hated how reedy her voice sounded. "I'll have to look it up later."

"I'd recommend that." Liesel fixed a pale, steely gaze on her for the longest second ever. "The article did also mention that you were a school teacher like the much-loved Princess Diana." Her voice rose to a mocking tone at the princess's name. "And I think we all know what happened to her. Her husband didn't really love her. He was in love with someone else all along." The last words were whispered so low they sounded almost like a hiss. Liesel rose to her feet and walked away.

Emma resisted the urge to breathe an audible sigh of relief, then glanced around her to gauge how many other people might have heard their exchange. Luckily, everyone around her was eating and talking. She glanced down at her plate, dismayed that her ravenous appetite had completely vanished.

Was Darias in love with someone else? Someone he couldn't marry because of royal protocol? She hadn't seen any obvious candidates in her quick Internet tour through his past, but that could be because there were pictures of him with so many different women.

Insecurity reared its ugly head. Of course she didn't expect him to actually love her. She was just a Jersey girl, after all. The term made her want to shake her head. What was wrong with being from New Jersey, for crying out loud? Nothing. That's what.

She stabbed her ham with her fork and cut it, then

tried to eat it, but it tasted like paper now that she wasn't hungry. Maybe she could find some way to keep busy, preferably away from the prying eyes of all these people trying to find fault with her. She could feel their gaze on her and she'd never felt more self-conscious in her life. Not even during the wedding when she knew everyone was staring at her.

She glimpsed Darias on the far side of the room. Her heart leapt for a second, then she realized he was probably busy and wouldn't relish being interrupted. Things were way more awkward now that she'd slept with him. At least before she knew where she stood. Now she had blissful moments where she felt like his real wife, followed by grim reminders that she was essentially a paid companion.

He looked up and their eyes met. For a second she was embarrassed at being caught staring, but he started to walk toward her, so she made another attempt at eating her breakfast.

He pulled up a chair and leaned in. "I'm going to join the Cross of Blood." He spoke so low she barely heard him over the hum of conversations around them.

"Why?"

"It's the only way I'll find out whose in it and what they're really up to. The attacker from yesterday said that his goal was to make me join."

"Then aren't you playing into his hands?" The idea horrified her. What if they just wanted to get him alone in some remote country house so they could.... Her mind boggled with hideous images.

"I don't see another route. It's a closed group. Influential people, aristocrats, very exclusive. They've been around for hundreds of years but there so cloaked in secrecy that no one outside of it seems to know what its all about. I need to find out what their purpose is. If they killed my father and grandmother—which right now I firmly believe they did—I need to find out why and bring the killer or killers to justice."

She swallowed. "I certainly understand your motivation, but it's too dangerous. Are you going to be armed?"

"I'm sure that if the Cross of Blood wanted me dead they'd figure out a way to do it right here, right now, in the palace dining room." He glanced up from their hushed conversation. "So I can only assume that they have other intentions for me. I'd be a coward if I didn't try to find out what they are." His dark eyes flashed with determination.

"How do you join?"

"Good question. I think I'll have a chat with Lorenzo Aldobrando."

"You should ask Beatriz if she learned anything from him."

"I did. She was infuriatingly mysterious. But that's not so unusual for her. I hardly imagine she'd let herself be seduced by the scion of one of our oldest rivals."

"Isn't that how they used to settle disputes in the old days?"

Darias's eyes narrowed. "Perish the thought."

By the next day most of the guests had left and the palace started to sink back into its quieter rhythms. Darias approached his mom about his intention of moving to the castle, and to his surprise she was warmly enthusiastic.

"It is the ancient seat of our kings." Carolina looked up from signing thank you notes for the lavish gifts she'd been given at the coronation. "I think it's only appropriate that you follow your grandmother's lead and take up residence there. I'd imagine you'll want some renovations. She could be very old fashioned about some things."

"It's fine for now. And Emma and I will enjoy the privacy afforded by a smaller household. Of course, we'll come visit you all the time and you're always welcome to come over." Emma loved how he always worried about his mom's feelings.

"I do appreciate that, my love. And I especially look forward to helping out when you have a new baby." She smiled in happy anticipation.

Darias's face fell fast, as did Emma's stomach. It had never crossed her mind that anyone would start hinting they should have a baby. And Darias looked appalled by the idea.

"Uh, Emma and I want to enjoy marriage and settle into our new lives for quite some time before we—"

"We're not quite ready yet." She joined in, hoping to make him sound more authentic. She hated the idea that his mom was dreaming of cute baby outfits and first words and had no prospect of getting them. One more thing to feel bad about when their one-year term ended.

She'd miss Carolina, too. It was still kind of weird calling her Mama on the rare occasions when it was totally unavoidable, but in some ways Carolina had already come to feel like a second mom, especially now that her own was gone. She was such a warm and kind woman, and still very beautiful, that Emma couldn't help hoping she'd find a new man and fall in love again, rather than trying to live vicariously through her children—which was usually a recipe for disappointment.

Speaking of which, she wondered if they'd found Jonas yet. Probably not. They'd have called if they had, wouldn't they? She walked to the side of the room, picked up her phone and scrolled through her messages, then cursed herself for having missed several new ones, partly because she had so many unread ones still sitting on her phone that she couldn't bring herself to read and respond to.

"Jonas found. Undergoing detox. Please call."

"Please excuse me." She walked outside the palace drawing room and called back. "It's Emma...Leone." Okay, that was weird. "Jonas Ricci is my brother. Is he okay?"

"Please hold for a moment." The receptionists tense voice sent Emma's pulse into overdrive. Had something happened to Jonas? She paced back and forth on the shiny marble floor.

"Ms. Leone, this is Doctor Fleiss. I'm afraid Jonas is rather ill. He had ingested a cocktail of substances, and we haven't yet unraveled what they are. He was unconscious when he was brought in."

"Oh, no! Has he regained consciousness?"

"Yes, but he's acting delirious. We'll know more as the drugs leave his system. You do know that he left of his own accord?"

"Of course. I know it was his own fault." Were they going to kick him out? She couldn't stay there in Altaleone if he would be released on his own— obviously very stupid—recognizance in New York. But how could she leave?

She was in a really difficult and pointless situation if

Jonas refused to stay in rehab. And what had he done to himself? Would he even recover? "Can he stay?"

"Of course. We'll update you with his progress but do call any time." The words were welcoming but the tone rather dismissive. After she hung up Emma found herself shaking so hard she could barely hold her phone.

"What's the matter?" Darias's concerned voice startled her.

"It's Jonas." She glanced toward the drawing room doorway. It was bad enough that his family had learned her brother was a junkie; they didn't need to know this latest wrinkle. "He got out of The Fountains and took drugs. He's back there now but very ill."

"You want to go to him, don't you?"

She bit her lip. "He doesn't deserve anyone to care about him. I tell myself that, but he's my brother...you know?"

"Of course." Darias put his hands on her shoulders. "We can fly to New York together."

"What? You've only just been crowned king. I'm sure that would cause kind of a scandal."

"We don't have to tell anyone the reason. We can blame my art career."

"Which would be a whole other scandal." She wanted to laugh. "Who ever heard of a king who makes art?"

"It's hard to imagine I'm the first." He looked rueful. "I suppose the other ones were wily enough to do it in secret."

"Let's wait and see how things pan out. He's detoxing—again—and I guess once the drugs are out of his system they can see how much damage has been done." She said a silent prayer that Jonas hadn't used all nine lives that he seemed to have. "It's not the first time he's nearly killed us with worry. He had a motorcycle crash when he was eighteen and broke his back. It was the prescription painkillers that got him started on drugs."

"Poor baby. You've been through a lot. I wish I could just lift all your burdens." The affectionate term touched her. So far he'd certainly done his best to make her life smooth and easy, even if it wasn't really her life at all.

Then Darias frowned and she wondered what he was thinking. "Perhaps Jonas should come live here for a while. It's very unlikely he'll be able to find drugs in Altaleone, and we'll have all the family and staff to look after him."

Emma stared. "Here? To the palace?" He had to be kidding. "I'm sure your Aunt Liesel would love that." She spoke quietly so as not to be overheard by the sharp-tongued woman.

Darias laughed. "I'm sure she would. She might scare some sense into him. But seriously, think about it. In a situation like this it's best to be surrounded by family."

But they're not his family, she wanted to protest. She couldn't bring herself to, though. It was the most warm, generous and caring offer she'd ever heard in her life.

Shame she'd never take him up on it in a million years. Darias didn't know Jonas. Her brother was a loose cannon who'd have no trouble telling Liesel that she looked like a weasel in a wig, and he wouldn't hesitate to lift priceless objects from the palace collection if he thought he could get away with it.

And even if Darias thought there were no drugs in Altaleone, Jonas would be sure to find some anyway. He had a real talent for it.

She sighed. It was horrible to think such negative thoughts about her own brother, but she knew that at this point his only real hope was effective professional help. "That's the kindest offer I could imagine, but I know he's better off at The Fountains. It's a physical addiction. They have drugs and therapy to help him get past that. If he comes here now, he'll still be in the grip of it."

"I understand." He stroked her back softly, so tenderly she could imagine for a moment that he truly loved her—that they really were family. "What can we do to take your mind off it? Shall we choose some things for our new home from the local stores?"

"Okay." She managed a shaky smile. "That sounds nice. I think I need some air."

They spent the afternoon strolling through beautiful old Casteleone, choosing luxurious bedding from one ancient—yet very chic—store and towels and bathroom effects from another. They had lunch at a lovely outdoor café and shared a pastry while walking under an avenue of trees.

"It's a tough life, this royal thing," she joked, as she dusted pastry crumbs off her hands. "I don't know how you've managed for this long."

His mouth tipped into his familiar wry smile. "I've done my best to avoid it by living overseas, but I guess now I'm stuck with it. Unfortunately I'm expected to buy expensive things often to support the local economy. Speaking of which…"

And the next thing she knew he led her to the jeweler and bought her a gorgeous gold necklace with a tiny dove charm. She held her breath as he fastened it around her neck. "It was prettier before I put it on you," he said softly. "Your beauty rather eclipses everything around it."

"Flatterer," she teased. "If you talked like that in New Jersey, you might get a drink thrown at you."

"Maybe I'll have to try it some time."

It was hard to imagine her and Darias in New Jersey, though she couldn't figure out why. Surely they'd go to New York together sooner or later, even if just for his art. She could take him to visit her old neighborhood.

Or not.

"I want to paint you tonight."

"I'd like that." She relished the idea of being all alone with him in his private studio, away from prying eyes. "You need to set up a studio in the old castle."

"Truth. Let's go buy some supplies." And they headed off down another cobbled street toward an old art supply shop with a bowed glass window.

I'm living in a fairy tale, she thought, climbing the worn steps to the store.

"Darias!" A woman's voice made them both turn. "I have something for you."

She was tall, with long dark hair falling past her shoulders, dressed in a fitted yellow dress that made her look like a supermodel from the 1960s.

"Gemma." He sounded stunned. "I didn't know you were here."

"There's a lot you don't know." The stunning woman didn't even glance at Emma. Was this the long-lost love that Liesel hinted at?

Of course it isn't. Don't be ridiculous! Get over yourself and…

She stiffened as the woman gave Darias a warm kiss on the cheek. He hesitated for a moment before pulling back. "Gemma, meet my wife, Emma."

Emma tried to force a smile to her lips. It was creepy how their names sounded similar. Emma thrust out a hand to shake, but the other woman didn't move. She had a small package in her right hand. Emma pulled her hand back.

She didn't say nice to meet you, because for some reason—that she couldn't quite put her finger on—it wasn't.

"Gemma and I have known each other since we were both knee-high."

"I'm sorry I couldn't make it to the wedding or the coronation. I was on assignment in Kabul."

"Gemma's a foreign correspondent for a big Paris paper," Darias explained. "You'd have been bored by it, anyway. You never did like big occasions. Is this a wedding gift?"

She laughed. "No. And open it in private." She thrust the package at him. It was wrapped in black paper with a white ribbon. "I'll catch you later." She turned and left while Darias was still examining the package. He finally looked up to see her long, tanned legs striding away down the street.

"She was always a handful." He looked wistful.

Emma battled the green monster writhing to life inside her. "I wonder what she gave you?" She hoped he wouldn't really open it in private. She was burning to know what was in it.

"I don't know." He weighed the box with his hand.

"Too heavy to be cuff links."

"You should open it."

He lifted a brow. "I'm not so sure. I think I'll wait."

Emma could visualize a sex toy or a framed naughty picture of Gemma or— Her imagination was running away with her. "Okay. Shall we go in?" She looked back at the art supply shop, which Darias seemed to have forgotten about.

He stood, turning over the package in his hands. "I'm too curious." He plucked at the ribbon. Emma's heart rate quickened as he pulled the ribbon off and slid a finger inside the paper. She tried not to lean in and peek.

He pulled back the paper and opened the box.

A blistering expletive fell from his lips before he clapped the lid back on like all the evils of the world might escape. "Let's go."

19

Darias ran after Gemma, but she'd rounded a corner and when they got there, she'd disappeared. An old man crossed the street very slowly with a small white dog at his heels.

"Damn it!"

"What was it?"

Darias drew in a steadying breath. He didn't want to tell Emma. She might worry. Or worse yet, tell his mom.

It was so small, really, for an artifact that had caused so much trouble over the centuries. He could hold it in the palm of his hand—bright, pure gold inset with rough, uncut rubies.

He'd seen it once before. His grandmother had shown it to him when he was little, telling him it would one day be his. How had it left his grandmother's possession and fallen into the hands of Gemma Cressi?

This was his initiation into the Cross of Blood society. He'd never even spoken to anyone about it, but somehow they knew. He shoved the box down into the pocket of his jacket.

"Darias, what's going on?"

"Did you see it?" He wasn't sure how much she

already knew.

"No." Her lips were pale. She looked so cold he wanted to hug and kiss her until color rose to her cheeks.

But now wasn't the time. "I need to put this under lock and key."

"What is it?" Her voice rose on her repeated question.

Was it wrong of him to keep it a secret from her? Maybe she deserved to know. A man wasn't supposed to keep secrets from his wife. Was she his wife? Sometimes he wasn't sure. When they were alone in bed together she felt like she was—

He pulled the box from his pocket and lifted the lid. He watched her expression as she stared, then she surprised him by reaching into the box and picked up the cross and its heavy chain.

She laughed, shocking him. "She gave you this? When are you supposed to wear it?"

Now he laughed, too. So much tension, waiting to explode. "You think it's funny?"

"Well, yes. I thought she'd give you something intimate, a secret memento or something from your shared past."

"You thought she was my girlfriend?" He lifted a brow.

"Yes. What else would I think?"

He sighed. She had been his girlfriend, of course. Long ago. That was all in the distant past. Obviously, she now had a more official role to play. "She's not my girlfriend. She's some kind of...ambassador. This is the infamous Cross of Blood."

He closed the box and put it away. Somehow it felt dangerous to have it exposed to the air on a public street.

Emma watched him put the box back in his pocket. "I suppose this is part of your initiation into the group."

"Yes, except that I never told anyone except you that I planned to join it."

"I didn't tell anyone, either." She looked startled, as if accused.

"I know that. It is possible that I'm being spied on, of course. And perhaps we were overheard. I wasn't entirely secretive about something that would soon become known anyway. Still…" What did it mean that they were entrusting him with their most precious object? "They're obviously risk takers. This must be worth millions just for the value of such large rubies. I guess they don't think I'm going to skip town with it."

"People do know where to find you when you're the king. We should put it somewhere safe. Maybe the armory?"

Darias inhaled. "I'm not sure the royal guard is even aware that it ever left the armory in the first place. This needs to be a secret for now. Until I answer some questions. Every day I have more of them."

They started walking down the street. He could get art supplies any time. Right now he needed to get this hidden safely away somewhere in the old castle. "I'd like us to move in starting tomorrow. We can renovate later. I'll feel more secure in the old structure. It's harder to hide spyware in solid stone walls than it is in lathe and plaster."

"True, and there will be fewer people around."

"Will you be lonely?" He hadn't considered that she might be almost all alone there most days.

"I'll be fine. It will give me time to read, and I'll visit your mom regularly."

Darias was touched. "That's sweet of you to think of her."

She laughed. "I'm thinking of myself. I really enjoy her company. And perhaps I can do something to help with the schools here. I am a teacher after all. I don't want to burden you with figuring out how to keep me busy, though. I can work that out by myself."

His chest swelled with pride. Emma was way more than just a pretty girl who looked convincingly like a queen. She had noble qualities that anyone could admire. How funny that she made a much better queen than any of the wealthy, spoiled heiresses and "princesses" that had been shoved in his path over the years.

"I'm sure that whatever you choose to do it will be a blessing for Altaleone." They turned up the hill toward the castle. He could almost feel the ancient cross burning a hole in his pocket.

They had him now. By accepting it, he'd accepted a thrown gauntlet, a challenge.

The most important thing was to keep the rest of his family—including Emma—safe. And it was his duty as king to protect his own life and the future of Altaleone. That might be the trickiest part of all.

Emma tried to stay out of the way as staff moved their effects from the palace to the old castle. Halfway through, she remembered her contract still sitting on top of the wardrobe in her first room in the palace.

She had to get it now. Once they were moved out

she'd have no excuse to even go back up to the second floor of the palace. Right now she had the pretext of checking for missing items, even in the old room.

Darias was off somewhere meeting with someone, so she decided not to tell him. She grabbed her bag and headed out for the palace on foot. She realized as she was walking that this was her first solo voyage through the streets of Altaleone.

Without her royal husband as protection, people stared at her far more boldly. Two handsome young men even smiled and waved, and she wasn't at all sure how to respond. She could hardly just ignore them as if they were construction workers on the streets of NYC.

She smiled politely and kept walking. Fast.

At the palace she greeted the guards at the door, then headed upstairs, hoping not to run into any family members. Darias's siblings had mostly trickled back to their busy lives, but his mom and Beatriz were usually somewhere nearby.

No one. Good.

She turned and headed along the corridor. Which door was it? They all looked the same when they were closed. Possibly some were still occupied by lingering guests from the coronation. She remembered it was the third one, though.

Hesitating outside the door, she knocked. No answer. She looked in both directions and saw that no one was coming, then she tried the handle.

Damn. It was locked.

Reaching into her wallet she pulled out her old library card. Were there security cameras trained on this hallway? She couldn't see any. She shoved her card in between the door and the frame and slid it down. The lock popped to the side and she pushed the door open.

If anyone saw that they'd probably think that—in addition to being a Jersey girl with a junkie brother—she was a petty thief. She closed the door behind her and locked it. If the room was still bugged or under video surveillance, she'd be screwed. She hurried to the wardrobe, raised her arm up and stood on tiptoe so she could reach the top.

Ugh. There was a sort of parapet on the front of the wardrobe so the area behind it was lower. She hadn't realized that when she'd shoved the envelope up there. She groped around with her fingers but couldn't feel anything but raw, unvarnished wood.

She carried the chair from the dresser over to the wardrobe, removed her shoes, then stood—very gingerly—on it. The chair was antique and probably quite fragile. She hoped she didn't plummet through it.

Up a full two feet higher, she still couldn't feel the piece of paper. Was this the right room? She looked around. Yes. Same bedding, same pictures on the wall. This was definitely the place.

She leaned in further and felt again. Yes! She felt the corner of a piece of paper. She reached for it with her fingertips, leaning further and further in until she managed to get thumb and finger around it and grab it.

She pulled it back, gasping with relief and climbed very carefully down off the chair.

But when she looked at the paper, her heart almost stopped beating.

It wasn't the contract at all.

Between her thumb and finger she held a single sheet of white paper. Written on it in a thick black script were the words, "Your secret is safe with me." And a smiley face.

No signature.

Blood rushed to her brain. Was it a maid who'd cleaned the room and actually did intend to keep her secret? Was it a member of Gibran's staff or even Gibran himself?

Gibran did not seem like the smiley-face type.

Or was it someone who—contrary to their darkly inked promise—did not have her best interests at heart at all.

She folded the paper and shoved it into her jacket pocket, put the chair back, then rushed for the door, heart pounding. She scanned the hallway—no one—but she couldn't help a creepy sense of being watched as she hurried back downstairs.

"Emma!" Beatriz's voice made her jump inside her skin. "Where are you going so fast?"

Was it Beatriz? It wasn't her writing, though she could have disguised it.

Was it Gemma, the glamorous woman who'd handed Darias the box? Unlikely. How would she have gotten into the palace? Darias was so surprised to see her that she probably wasn't at the wedding or coronation celebrations.

Then who?

Possibly someone else from the mysterious Cross of Blood. Someone living or working right here in the palace, watching their every move and planning…. It could be nasty aunt Liesel who'd been needling her ever since she arrived.

She realized she hadn't even responded to Beatriz.

"Uh, just making sure we didn't leave anything behind in the move."

"Don't worry. It's not like we're turning the place over to the new owners later today. If you leave stuff behind you can come and get it tomorrow." Beatriz looked amused. Emma could swear her eyes wandered to her right jacket pocket, where the folded note lay—throbbing with guilt—below the thin fabric.

"Oh, I know. Just trying to be organized, I guess."

"Come join us. We were just about to go for a walk in the gardens. The gardener has created a new bed in honor of Darias taking the throne. He found heirloom roses dating back to the time Altaleone was founded."

"Uh," she scrambled to think of an excuse. And failed. These royals lived quite a life, spending their days planning grand parties and looking at flowers. And right now, that was her life. "Sure. That sounds great." She hoped she sounded more enthusiastic than she felt.

At least she didn't have the contract in her pocket, in which she agreed to accept cold hard cash to be a big phony in their midst for an entire year.

But someone knew about it.

Who?

And there was no avoiding it—now she had to tell Darias she'd lost the contract.

20

Darias knew that the Cross of Blood would soon be in touch again. They'd hardly hand over the prized icon and disappear back into the woodwork. He decided to make it easy for them by walking each journey between the palace and the castle. The security guards could hardly protest him having free run of his own country, though he knew they were never far away from him.

As expected, they didn't wait long. As he walked down the broadest avenue in Casteleone, watching a young boy throw a stick for his dog, an old beggar woman approached him and tugged at his clothes. He reached into his pocket for some cash, but as he tried to give it to her she thrust a folded piece of paper into his hand.

His eyes snapped into focus, studying her. She still looked like an old homeless woman. Which was odd since there was no homelessness in Altaleone. She stood there, watching him through rheumy eyes while he unfolded the thick paper and read the black handwritten script.

We will meet at the old summer palace at ten of the clock—night—on the last Thursday in the month of your coronation.

"No." He looked hard at her. "We will meet in the

old castle right here in Altaleone. Tell them that." He handed the paper back to her and watched her. She didn't say anything, or even nod but bowed her head slightly, then turned and shuffled slowly away.

As she reached the corner he watched her pick up her skirt and speed up. Probably not even someone old. He hated all this cloak-and-dagger bullshit. He wasn't a big fan of pomp and ceremony of any kind, but he'd grown to accept it as his birthright.

They were coming now, and he was ready.

Emma was pacing back and forth in the dim front hallway of the castle when the door flung open, flooding the space with light. She startled. "Oh, it's you."

Darias lifted a brow. "Who else were you expecting?" He approached her and circled his arms around her waist. Instead of relaxing into them, she felt herself stiffen. "I have something to tell you."

"You've taken a lover?" He pretended to glance nervously toward the door.

She laughed. Or tried to. "No, worse than that."

He looked doubtful. "Not to my mind." He stroked her cheek. "You're pale. What's going on?"

She swallowed, hoping he wouldn't be too furious. It was in the contract that she had to keep their arrangement secret, and by letting that piece of paper slip from her grasp, she'd broken her promise. "Someone knows about our arrangement."

She felt the breath rush from him, and he stepped back. "How?"

Suddenly cold without his arms around her, she shivered a little. "I brought our contract with me.

Stupid, I know…" Her voice was rising. "I should have left it at home in a bank or something, but I didn't realize there'd be staff going through our stuff and moving it around." She shoved a hand through her hair. "When I moved into my first room I shoved it up on top of the wardrobe. When I finally got a chance to retrieve it this afternoon, it was gone and had been replaced with a note saying that someone knew my secret."

"Damn." Darias's face looked grim. He looked right past her, frowning. Then his dark eyes focused on hers. "I need to find out who it was. Do you have the paper?"

She nodded. Then turned to retrieve it from a little locked cabinet in the room they'd chosen as her study. She'd hidden it in a boring-looking manila envelope labeled *notes*.

She pulled it out, holding it as if it were burning hot, and held it out to him. "I've tried not to touch it. I know it might have fingerprints."

Darias took it gingerly. "Yes. Thing is, I don't want Gibran and his crew to know about our arrangement either. I don't want anyone to know—ever." His eyes met hers again, with breath stealing force. "Someone could challenge my right to the throne if they knew our marriage isn't real."

Our marriage isn't real. The words were hardly a surprise, but they still hit her like a bucketful of icy water.

"I know. I've been in a panic since I found it. I'm sure we can find out who stayed in that room during the coronation."

"It was there the entire time, since we arrived until when?"

"I don't know when it was found and the note substituted for it. I didn't get a chance to check until today."

"That's nearly three weeks."

"I know. I'm so, so sorry. I feel like an idiot for leaving it exposed."

"Don't blame yourself. I should have asked you if you had anything that needed to be hidden. It's my fault." He wasn't looking at her but down at the enigmatic paper. "For now we'll keep it hidden and keep our eyes and ears peeled. I need to figure out what's going on with this Cross of Blood society."

"Do you think the two are connected?"

"Honestly, I have no idea." He folded the paper. "They gave me a note today. Different writing and paper, though."

"Where is it?"

"I gave it back to the messenger. They wanted to meet me at the old summer palace where my father and grandmother were murdered in cold blood." He let out a savage laugh. "They must think I'm an idiot."

"You told them no." She said it as a statement, praying it was true.

"I told them to meet me here."

"What?" She felt her eyes widen. "In our home?"

He looked apologetic for a split second. "I need to meet them on my turf. Here I can record the whole thing if necessary—not that it will help since they're bound to wear masks—and they'll know I have security on hand if not in the room. If they're going to kill me here, I can at least make it damn difficult for them."

The castle was from an early enough era that it had been built to keep marauders out rather than provide a comfortable habitat, so the windows were small and the walls solid stone rather than smooth plaster. Still, as they settled in, moved the furniture into more comfortable arrangements and added fun antiques and knickknacks from the stores around Altaleone, it began to feel like a home of sorts. Yes, she wasn't going to be there forever, but she'd lived all her life in rentals so that was hardly odd.

Did it hurt that she'd be leaving all the treasures she and Darias were gathering to furnish their shared life? Not really.

It would hurt to leave Darias, though. She couldn't deny that. Each night they made love and slept in each other's arms like a real married couple who had their whole lives ahead of them to share.

Each morning she had to peel herself away from his warm, muscled body, and it felt a bit like ripping off a Band-Aid because she knew that each morning was bringing them closer to the day she'd get up and pack her bags and say good-bye.

"It's Thursday today." Darias's gruff voice was half muffled by the pillow. She lay still, with his arm draped over her. "The cook is preparing some food for our *guests*—" He said the word with a hint of mockery. "As I intend to be a perfect host."

"Are you scared?"

"No." He sat up, then turned to her with a serious expression. "Though I quite understand if you don't want to greet them."

"I'll be there if you like."

"It would be nice to have a second pair of eyes on them. I imagine they'll all be masked or otherwise disguised. I want to figure out who they all are."

"I doubt I'll know any of them." Sometimes she felt pretty useless there in Altaleone. If they didn't speak English, she wouldn't even understand them.

"You never know. You've met a lot of people since you came here, what with us hosting the two biggest parties of the twenty-first century."

"True." She bit her lip. "What do you wear to a secret society meeting?"

Darias laughed, sitting up. "Whatever you damn well please."

"Maybe I should find a robe and mask of some kind."

"That would be a terrible waste of your beauty." He grinned, looking her up and down in a way that made her skin sizzle. "But would likely serve them right." He stood up and stretched. "But after we have hors d'oeuvres, you should disappear. Go barricade yourself in our bedroom. It's completely secure. I've had the locks beefed up, and the walls are solid stone nearly two feet thick, built to protect a queen."

"Will there be guards here?"

"When I want them. If I want them gone, they'll be gone. I plan to let events unfold and react accordingly."

Emma's stomach tightened. "What if they..." Could she even say it aloud? "What if they try to kill you?"

"I suppose if they all jump on me with broadswords there won't be a lot I can do. But I can't live in fear. If they all want me dead for some obscure reason, then eventually they'll succeed. My main goal right now is finding out who killed my family and avenging their deaths."

She shivered slightly. She didn't want to ask what

kind of vengeance he'd seek. "I understand." She climbed out of bed. "I'll try to be a keen observer. Just give me a hint when it's time for me to leave."

Darias didn't say anything. He moved toward her, gorgeously naked, and took her in his arms. He kissed her softly on the lips, then deepened the pressure until her breath came in ragged gasps and her nipples pushed against his chest.

I love him.

The thought assaulted her mind as his tongue plundered her mouth. If he could be brave, then she could be brave for him. She might be a queen in name only, but she would do her best to think and act like one tonight.

With Darias's encouragement Emma wore a long blue dress that had belonged to his grandmother. The older woman was several inches shorter, so the dress fell to ankle length, where it brushed against a pair of mock snakeskin ankle boots they'd bought in New York. She pinned a strange but intriguing pin of a dragonlike creature at the neckline. The overall look was cocktail party chic mixed with secret-society drama.

Darias wore all black, hardly unusual for him, but although he seemed outwardly relaxed she sensed a certain tautness about him, like a freshly tuned string. The staff, including several of Gibran's men—some of whom were women—were instructed to stay out of the way unless summoned. They had a code if immediate entry or rescue of some kind was required, and although Darias had pooh-poohed the idea of panic buttons, Gibran's insistence that they also protected Emma had convinced him to set at least one carefully hidden but easily reachable one in each room they might enter.

Hidden cameras were set up to record everything. "If I can't figure out who they are tonight, I'll watch the footage and unravel the mystery later," said Darias.

The first guest arrived about five minutes early. Emma wasn't sure if they'd all show up in a mob, so she was relieved when only one figure emerged from the black Mercedes she saw arrive in the castle courtyard.

Her gut clenched when she saw their "guest" emerge wearing a mask, even though she'd been told to expect that. It was a woman, dressed in a long black tunic with a hood that covered her hair. Her mask was black and silver and covered most of her face. Emma could only tell she was a woman from the way she carried herself.

"A pleasure to meet your majesty," she said—in barely accented English—as she kissed Emma's hand. Her own hands were gloved. "And warm greetings to our new king."

Emma watched her eyes sparkle behind the mask as she moved toward Darias. Was it the same woman who gave him the cross? She couldn't tell. She was tall enough. Emma suppressed a little green flash of jealousy.

"I would greet you warmly myself, but it's difficult when I don't know who you are." Darias looked intrigued by their visitor. Maybe he'd been expecting a gathering of old men.

"Who I am doesn't matter." She took the glass of wine Darias offered. "I am simply one of many who want to secure the future of our cause."

Emma was dying to ask, "What is your cause?" but

managed to hold her tongue. It probably had something to do with the Holy Grail. Or a numbered Swiss bank account. Or both.

The ancient knocker on the door rapped again—a rather terrifying sound—and Emma walked over to open it. Now two men, one tall and one short, both in long cloaks and masks, greeted her. Another three came behind them. With this many people you'd normally expect a hum of conversation to fill the room, but apart from the formal greetings, they remained silent.

They could hardly chitchat among each other and keep their identities secret.

"Are we all here?" asked Darias. He was the tallest and maintained a commanding air of authority despite being the only one not in costume.

"We are," said an older man. "Thank you for hosting us."

"I'm sure you know why I invited you here. I want to know who killed my father and grandmother."

An odd silence followed his statement.

"So do we." The older man. "Our sworn duty is to protect the monarchy of Altaleone and the sacred legacy of the Holy Roman emperors."

"You screwed up big-time, then." Darias's voice grew louder. Emma tried not to stare. She could see that he didn't believe them. "What was with the kinky sex vibe of the murders?"

There was a pause. The man cleared his throat. "You were not aware that they had...proclivities?"

"Proclivities?" Darias spat the word. "No. I certainly was not, and I don't believe it now. My grandmother was nearly eighty."

"Age does not preclude desire," said the young

woman who'd arrived first, in a crisp, clear tone. "Perhaps you didn't know them as well as you thought."

Darias stared at them, and Emma could almost feel waves of rage rolling off him. Her adrenaline started to run and she glanced around, wondering if she should offer them wine, or the now ridiculous-looking hors d'oeuvres on silver plates on the sideboard.

"Emma, would you mind leaving us?" His soft tone sounded forced.

"Of course." Relief mingled with anxiety for Darias. Was it really good to leave him alone—and getting mad—in a room full of masked weirdos?

Still, she'd promised, so she headed upstairs and—also as promised—locked the door and texted Gibran's team that she was there.

The whole thing is being videotaped. Of course that wouldn't be much consolation if they had great footage of Darias being murdered.

She paced back and forth across the room, wishing she could hear what was being said downstairs. The walls and floors were too thick, and their bedroom was too far away.

Darias clenched his fists, willing himself to keep his temper under control. He had a long, slow fuse, but once lit it could be fiercely explosive. "Who are you?" First he asked the assembled group of masked strangers. Then he zeroed in on the older man who'd spoken. "Who are *you*?"

"Who I am doesn't matter." His voice was quiet. "We exist only to protect you and the sacred legacy."

"Well, after what happened to my forebears I think it

may be time for you to retire." He couldn't hide the disgust in his voice. "We'll stick with hired security from now on."

"We have reason to believe you are in grave danger."

"It doesn't take a rocket scientist to figure that out." He felt his eyes narrow. "Which one of you is Lorenzo Aldobrando?" He scanned the group, looking for the arrogant young man who'd dared to flirt with his sister.

Silence greeted him.

"He is not among us." An older woman spoke. "He has never been one of us."

Interesting. "Perhaps I can discover your identities through a process of elimination." He already had an idea about the older man. He sounded like a friend of his father's who'd shared his passion for vintage Italian race cars.

"What exactly do you do to protect the monarchy and the…" He stopped himself before saying *sacred legacy* with a sneer in his voice.

"Not enough, clearly," said a man who sounded about Darias's own age. "There have always been forces around Altaleone—other nations at our borders, landowners, business rivals, those who seek our riches. In a global economy, perhaps the legion of enemies has grown while we've slept."

Darias lifted a brow. "There are probably more cutthroats on one block in New York City than in all of Altaleone."

"It only takes one," said the young woman.

"You think one person murdered my father and grandmother?"

There was a pause. "No." Another man spoke. "We think there were at least two. We think they were murdered at the same time."

"Seduced, according to their…proclivities, then murdered?"

"Yes."

"Why would they allow someone to lead them into such a ridiculous predicament?"

"They thought they were among us."

21

Darias stared around the group. "They thought they were going to…" He couldn't finish the sentence because he had no idea what he would say.

"We have…rituals. We're a very exclusive group." The older woman. "All of us belong to the region's aristocracy, and we are sworn to secrecy until we die—or members of the group will dispatch us to death."

The older man stepped forward. "It's not easy for royals to enjoy the pleasures that others take for granted, so we provide a safe environment for mutual enjoyment."

Darias felt his hackles rising again. "So this whole secret cloak-and-dagger society is really just a kinky sex club?"

"No." An older man spoke quietly. "It's more than that. It's for the nourishment and protection of the monarchy."

"Well, I can protect myself, thanks, so I think I'm going to turn in my membership." He wished he had that damned ruby cross right here so he could throw it at them. "Listen, I don't have any problem with people exploring their desires and doing whatever they want on their own time, but I have no interest in that kind of thing and clearly your role as bodyguards is lacking. So I'll take it from here."

He wondered how to gracefully show a group of people out the door.

But damn it, he still hadn't figured out who most of them were. He needed more footage.

"We need to protect you. It's our sworn duty."

He wondered if—as monarch—he could insist they dispatch each other to death for failing in their duty to his dad and grandma. "And how do you propose to do that?"

"Has anyone contacted you?" The oldest man.

"Everyone in the goddamn world has contacted me. I just got married and crowned king."

The masked man cleared his throat. "Anyone...of interest."

"Well, there was the man with a firework who threw himself in front of my carriage. And my wife opened a mysterious note. My security chief recognized it as being from a French text, threatening something or other."

"Do you remember the words?" The young woman.

Darias sighed. "The queen is gone, her secrets kept / Her son so close behind her / The brave new heir does hope to rule / But battle brings the sound of thunder." He stared at them, daring them to find meaning in the pointless old words.

The older man straightened his back. "Distracted by a maiden fair, the king will lose his all."

"And tyranny will rule the lands again before the fall," continued the young woman.

"You all know this poem?" Darias found that odd. "It's not even from Altaleone. It's French."

"Not all of us, perhaps," said the older man. "But it is part of our educational legacy. It was written for your ancestor Charlemagne."

"Ah." Everything came back to Charlemagne sooner or later. Sometimes Darias wished he'd had less illustrious forebears. "I can assure you that I'm not distracted by a maiden fair, despite appearances to the contrary. And why did you send someone to jump in front of my carriage? You could have injured her or myself."

"We didn't." At least two of them spoke at once.

"What?" He frowned. "But he said—"

"That he wanted you to join us?" The young woman again.

"Yes. And frankly, that was when I decided that I needed to. If you didn't know that, how did you send Gemma Cressi with the cross."

"Gemma is not one of us either. The cross was stolen at the time of the murders."

Now Darias stared. "So they're both part of some criminal conspiracy?"

Or these people are.

"Take off your masks. As your king, I command you."

Emma had changed out of her dress and into pajamas, but she couldn't relax enough to go to bed. Or even sit down in a chair. Yes, she'd promised to stay out of the way, but how could she leave Darias alone down there with a bunch of masked strangers who might have murdered his family members?

Maybe she could just sneak back and peek through the keyhole. Sure, her movements might well be recorded on a hidden video camera set up somewhere, but it wasn't like she was planning to do anything criminal or even bad.

She just cared about her husband.

"My husband." She said it aloud, feeling for the strangeness of the word. Was he really her husband, even for a year, when the vows they'd so carefully repeated were merely part of a contractual obligation?

The more time they spent together—sleeping in each other's arms like a real husband and wife—the more he felt like her husband where it counted, in her heart.

Damn it, I am going down there. She couldn't stay locked up there when he might be getting his throat slit, or worse.

She dressed again, this time in black leggings and a black top, like a cat burglar. She put on her quietest sneakers and tied her hair in a braid down her back. If anyone surprised her, she'd say she was looking for her book. This was her home, after all.

Heart thumping so loud she could practically hear it, she eased out of the bedroom and crept toward the stairs. Luckily, the stone steps would never creak, so she hurried down with confidence, then paused to listen at the bottom.

She could hear voices coming from the great hall, even though all the doors to it were now closed. She couldn't tell what they were saying, though. She couldn't even understand it. As she moved closer, ears pricked, she realized they were now speaking in a different language, probably the local dialect of Altaleone, which was a confusing hybrid of Italian and German.

The door she'd left through was ancient, made of carved oak boards, and had a good-sized keyhole, with no key in it since the doors had all been fitted with a latch at some point in the twentieth century.

She snuck closer and lowered herself until she was eye level with the hole. Holding her breath, she leaned closer and peered in, and what she saw made a scream rise in her throat.

Darias lay on the long dining table in the middle of the room, and the masked and cloaked strangers stood around him, swords and daggers of various sizes in their raised hands, literally hovering over him, ready to plunge into him.

But what stopped her from screaming, or bursting through the door, was his expression. He looked calm, intrigued, even, studying their masked faces.

Emma cursed herself for not bringing her phone down with her. She couldn't call for help right now except with her own feeble voice. But would Darias want her to?

As she watched, heart now racing with terror, each of the masked men and women raised their left hand and pushed their mask back, revealing their face.

Her eyes raced around the group, hoping for recognition. She could swear she'd seen one of the middle-aged men before and the oldest woman looked familiar, but she couldn't place where she'd seen them. They must have been guests at either the wedding or the coronation, or both.

They still held their weapons high, as Darias looked around the group, dark eyes keen, drinking in all the information around him. They lowered their masks, covering their faces, then their blades.

"You've seen us now." The oldest man spoke in English again. "You trusted us not to kill you when we had the chance, and we trusted you with our identities. No one else must *ever* know who we are." He spoke the word *ever* with a chilling emphasis that made Emma shrink back from the keyhole, afraid the shine in her eye might give her away.

Why had Darias decided to trust them? One woman extended her hand, and Darias took it and raised himself up from the hard surface of the table. "Now I understand," he murmured, so low she could barely hear him. "Each of you has as much to lose as I do."

"We've all vowed to risk our lives to protect you," said a woman. Emma could still see her hauntingly beautiful face.

"And I pledge my silence to protect you." He sighed. "What should I do about the boy in my cells?"

"Let him go. Follow him to his source."

"Then I lose his value as a hostage."

"He has no value as a hostage if his life is no longer important to them. These people have killed a queen and her heir. We must assume life has little value to them. Let him show us who they are and what they want."

Darias nodded. "I'll have his movements

tracked."

"And don't assume they aren't doing the same to you with the cross."

Emma watched as Darias's face paled. It hadn't occurred to either of them that the ruby studded cross might have been tampered with.

"I appreciate the warning. How do I get in touch with you?"

"We will stay in touch with you." The oldest woman, who had piercing blue eyes and looked like a queen herself, at least she had during the brief glimpse that Emma had stolen of her. "For now we must leave. We can never stay anywhere so long that our absence from somewhere else is noticed and the identity of our group discovered.

They left much as they'd arrived, the remaining guests now hovering around the drinks and snacks but not eating them as their masks covered their whole faces, including their mouths. Emma reflected that the hole for speech was probably large enough to take a straw, but who drank wine with a straw?

She was getting punchy and her thoughts running away with her. She'd better get away before someone decided to try this door, which led upstairs into the castle. At least she'd been reassured that Darias—probably—wasn't about to be murdered, despite all appearances to the contrary.

She crept back upstairs as fast as she could and closed the bedroom door behind her.

When she heard footsteps on the stairs her heart quickened in anticipation of seeing Darias—then quickened further at the awful thought that it might be someone else.

She sat up in bed, pulling the covers around her as the lock clicked open. Relief rushed over her in a hot wave at the sight of Darias—larger than life and ten times as handsome—standing in the doorway.

"Thank goodness that's over!" She jumped out of bed, rushed toward him and threw her arms around him. "I was scared."

Darias kissed her and rubbed her warmly with his arms. "Nothing to be scared about. But interesting. Apparently, it wasn't they who gave me the gold cross…"

"I know. I was listening at the door." Her confession rushed out. She couldn't bear to lie to him.

"Why?"

"To make sure you were safe. I had my doubts when they all pulled swords and daggers on you."

A hollow laugh shook his chest. "That was an expression of mutual trust. These people are leaders and oligarchs from around our region— not just Altaleone. They see Altaleone as the keystone of peace and prosperity in our region— and are determined to protect the country and its monarchy at all costs. They want me to release the boy that threw the firework, then follow him to his source."

Her gut clenched at the idea of letting someone with evil intentions go free. "I suspect that's what he wants, too. He told you to join the Cross of Blood, and you did. Doesn't it seem a bit fishy?"

"No doubt. But I can't just sit around waiting for the killer to fall into my lap. I need to take action." He hugged her tight. "I'll keep you safe, I promise."

"I'm more worried about you being safe." She held him close, feeling the powerful beat of his brave heart.

"Don't worry about me." He kissed her again, extending it until heat flushed her core. "I can take care of myself." He stroked her cheek. "But for now, I want to take care of you." He slid his fingers lower, cupping her behind and nodding toward the bed.

And he did. He made love to her with slow precision—delicate work with fingers, lips and tongue—making her wait until she was practically panting and begging him to enter her. Then he slid inside her and moved just slowly enough to drive her almost to the brink of madness. Somehow he managed to find pleasure centers that she never knew existed.

When they finally came—always together—the explosive relief was so intense she could hardly breathe.

I love you, Darias. Once again, she managed not to say it. She knew instinctively that the confession would be too much and would drive him away. Their whole relationship rested on her knowing her place—really, she was a high-paid royal mistress, in a long tradition of kept women—and not stepping outside the bounds.

Even if it almost killed her.

When Darias went to the bathroom to clean up, she noticed that her phone was flashing. She must have missed a call while she was downstairs, then been too distracted and nervous to notice it when she came up. She pressed the button and listened to a message. Her heart swelled at the sound of her brother's voice.

"Hey, sis, I miss you." Her breath caught at the sound of his warm admission. She couldn't even remember the last time he'd said something nice to her. "My treatment's going well, but I'm getting kind of restless in here. They seem to want me to stay almost forever, but you know me, I'm kind of a rolling stone."

Yeah, that's the problem. Her gut clenched at the thought of him checking himself out.

"Anyway, call me when you get the chance."

"Is that your brother?" Darias asked, as he emerged from the bathroom, skin sparkling with fresh droplets from the shower.

"Yes, he wants to check himself out. Which is a terrible idea. He hasn't been sober long enough to have formed new habits."

"Let's bring him here. Then we can keep a close eye on him and make sure he doesn't drink or use drugs." Darias toweled himself, displaying a distracting amount of rippling bicep and pectoral.

"I really don't think so." Everything in her recoiled at the prospect. "He's…unpredictable."

"He's family." Darias didn't look worried. "We'll manage."

"But he's not…" *Not really family. I'm not really family. I'm just here for a year and then—* "I'll call him tomorrow and see if I can find out what's going on."

"All right, beautiful." He hung his towel and climbed into bed. When he wrapped his arms around her, she forgot about her brother and the contract and everything else as she drifted to sleep in his arms.

"What is the meaning of this?" Liesel stood up and waved a newspaper at Emma and Darias as they arrived at the palace—their former home—for lunch.

"Liesel," half-whispered Darias's mom. "Don't."

"The meaning of what?" Darias strode forward, sounding as if he didn't care much either way.

"You let him go! The man who tried to kill you."

"I have my reasons." He pulled back a chair for Emma, and she sat in it.

"He's an enemy of the crown." Liesel looked scandalized.

"True, but it's my crown so I must decide how to handle its enemies." Darias kissed his mom on the cheek before sitting between her and Emma. "And it suits my purposes to let him go."

"Well, don't blame me if you're found dead tomorrow." Liesel was clearly fuming. Emma wondered why she cared so much. Maybe she just enjoyed having something to fuss and scold over.

"Emma and I have finally settled in enough to entertain at the old castle, so we'd like to invite you all over for little party on Saturday."

His mom's face burst into a smile. "That's wonderful! I can't wait to see what you've done with it. Are we all invited?" She cast a doubtful glance at her sister.

"Of course. And I've invited all of us."

"Your brothers and sisters?"

"Yes, though I don't know how many will be able to get away when they were here so recently."

"That's wonderful. I'm so glad you're making an effort to get the family together regularly. I'd begun to feel you were all going to just drift away from me."

A waiter passed around three different salads and some sliced chicken or duck.

"I apologize for spending so much time in New York over the last few years. I was so caught up in my art career and my life there that I almost forgot how my behavior must have looked from this side of the Atlantic."

His mom waved her hand dismissively. "You know I was proud of you every moment, Darias. And so was your father."

Emma's phone rang, and she glanced at it. "Oh, it's my brother. I'd better take it." She excused herself and hurried out into the hallway. "Jonas, are you okay?"

"Never better, sis. I'm ready to be sprung."

"I don't think that's a great idea. You've only been there a few weeks. And you had a relapse, remember?" She thought about what Darias had suggested. And rejected the idea out of hand. Jonas was far too unpredictable to be let loose in a royal household. She couldn't even imagine what he'd reply to Liesel if she made one of her habitual sharp comments to him. "Let me see if I can come visit and talk to the doctors. We'll see what they recommend." She wasn't sure if that was even a possibility, but at least it would hold him there while she figured out what to do.

"Sis, I'm dying of boredom here! People sit around watching TV all day. They're actually desperate enough to play board games."

"You used to love playing chess when we were kids."

"Only so I could win your allowance from you."

She laughed at the memory. He used to spend it all on candy, then cigarettes, then party drugs.... Her smile faded. "Do you promise me that you'll stay there a few more days?"

He let out a forced sigh. "If I have to."

"It's really important to me."

"Yes, your royal majesty." He let out a loud laugh. "You really are the goddam queen, aren't you? I saw it on TV. One of those stupid gossip shows they love in here. You had a fricking crown on your head."

She bit her lip. She couldn't explain the situation to Jonas. She'd only had the crown on her head for a few minutes for an official photo before it was hurried back to the armory. "I am. It's not as weird as it seems. It's sort of a ceremonial job."

"You have to let the peasants kiss your hands?"

"There aren't any peasants. Altaleone is very wealthy. People here all earn money from the state."

"Like in Kuwait? Sweet. I think I'd like it there."

Panic flared in her chest. "You'd find it very dull." *There are no drugs, for one thing.*

"It might be just what I need. It would do me good to get away from New York and all the bad influences here."

"Uh, I suppose it might. Still…"

"You're afraid I'll embarrass you, aren't you?"

Yes. "No! I'm just…I'm new around here myself and trying to learn the ropes. If you're really interested in coming here, I'll talk to Darias about it, though."

"I'm sure he'd be just thrilled to entertain your junkie brother in his royal palace."

His rudeness made her indignant. "Actually he suggested it himself. He thinks you *should* come here."

"And I agree. Can I fly direct or do I have to change somewhere?"

The ball started rolling and just kept picking up speed and steam until her brother was released from The Fountains and booked on a flight to Paris, from where he'd catch a shuttle to Casteleone.

On Saturday, the morning of their planned party at the castle, she took a car to meet him at the small local airport. When he got off the plane, she barely recognized him.

22

"Jonas," she kissed him on the cheek, which, for the first time in years, was clean-shaven. His blue eyes shone bright and his hair was neatly cut and he looked alert and alive and.... "I can't believe this. You look amazing."

"Feel pretty good, too. Clean and sober."

"I'm thrilled." The misgivings about having him here, which had been breeding in her heart for days, began to subside. She'd started out on this crazy journey hoping that The Fountains would deliver her brother from his druggy prison and give him back to her, and against all the odds it really seemed to be happening. "Wait, don't move, let me hug you again!"

Jonas and Darias had met before, of course, under less than ideal circumstances, so she felt so proud to reintroduce her newly awakened sibling to him. Darias welcomed him warmly and invited him to stay as long as he wanted.

As the guests arrived for their party—a sort of outdoor picnic with a live guitarist and singer, Emma found herself relaxing. Nearly all of Darias's siblings had flown in, keen to see what they'd done to the gloomy old castle, and Jonas handled the introductions with ease and charmed even the prickly Liesel with a compliment about the antique brooch she wore.

They sat on the castle terraces and lawns, listening to music and eating delicious gourmet picnic food. "Isn't this great?" asked Darias to no one in particular. "Our family lost two members this year and now we've gained two."

Emma stared. Did he really mean it? That they were actually family? Not just for a year but in a truly permanent way?

She didn't dare to let her mind wander too far down that track. She toasted his announcement, wondering how his family would feel if they knew the coldhearted business arrangement that had brought her there.

Her heart wasn't cold anymore, though. It filled with love as she watched Darias interact with his siblings, whom he clearly adored. He played an athletic game of badminton with the two youngest, Leo, short for Leopold, and Lina—who was named after their mother, Carolina. They were both on summer break from their respective colleges and had flown in following a short trip to the South of France.

Lina was bubbly and sweet and laughed uproariously at Jonas's account of trying to help an elderly lady get her bag off the airport baggage claim conveyer and being attacked by her as a thief.

After lunch they sat around chatting. Emma relished the opportunity to relax and get to know Darias's siblings better without the pressure and formality around the wedding and the coronation.

They no longer seemed like a sea of strange faces but each a warm and intriguing individual in their own right. Even Beatriz seemed relaxed, though Emma stiffened every time Beatriz glanced in her direction. Emma strongly suspected her of leaving the note with the smiley face. Still, she hadn't told anyone about it...yet.

Darias's tall and frighteningly handsome brother, Rigo, an outspoken lawyer, held them spellbound with his account of his latest case that combined both large-scale water pollution and organized crime, and the sun was almost setting before she realized how late it had grown.

Where's Jonas? She hadn't seen him for a while. He'd settled so easily into the group—she'd almost forgotten what a charmer he could be when he wasn't jonesing for a fix—that she'd stopped worrying about him hours ago.

Now she couldn't see him anywhere.

"Excuse me for a moment." She ducked out of a conversation with Darias's mom and his sister Cosima. "I'll be right back."

She scanned the neatly landscaped castle garden—there wasn't all that much of it—as she headed for the big door to the castle's cool, dark interior. She saw most of the other party attendees but not Jonas. Already her stomach clenched. Had he snuck out to buy drugs?

She picked up the pace once out of sight inside the castle keep. He wasn't in the great hall or the smaller sitting rooms and studies off it. She pulled her phone from her pocket and texted him.

Where are you?

No answer. Doubting herself, she climbed the

stairs. The castle didn't have that many bedrooms. In ancient times the servants must have lived in town. There were four big ones on the same floor as hers and Darias's, and two further smaller ones up behind the battlements.

The first four stood empty, but she thought she heard an unfamiliar noise. She climbed the stairs. "Hello?"

Silence. She paused a moment. Why would anyone be upstairs? Still, she kept going. The first door opened on an empty room with a bare, unmade mattress. The second...the door was locked.

She hadn't locked it, and the maid only cleaned up here once a week. She'd been in there since to place a new vase she'd bought for the deep windowsill.

She knocked. "Hello?"

A rustling sound made her ears prick up.

"Who's there?"

Silence.

"I know there's someone in there. Jonas, is it you?" She remembered that she had a skeleton key to all the new locks in the castle, and she ran back to her room to get it, then rushed back upstairs. As soon as she put it in the lock and turned it, she heard her brother's voice.

"Can't I get a little privacy?" She pushed the door open to see him pulling his pants on, but her eyes immediately flew to the other person in the room—Darias's youngest sister Lina—who was struggling to do up her bra, face crimson with embarrassment.

"What is going on?"

"Really?" Her brother lifted a sardonic brow. "Don't be dense."

"She's a child, Jonas."

"No, I'm not," she protested with a pout. "I'm in college. You don't think I was a virgin, do you?"

Emma blinked, speechless. "Uh, I suppose not. But this is not...Jonas! I can't believe this."

"Really? Then you don't know me as well as you think you do."

"Do you realize"—now she was looking at Lina—"that Jonas just got out of drug rehab? That he's still in a very fragile state?"

Lina blinked. "I didn't know that."

"No, I don't suppose he told you, either."

Jonas shrugged, tucking his band tee into his jeans and buckling the leather belt. "She'd probably have jumped into bed quicker if I had. Girls love fixing a bad boy." He winked at Lina, who had the decency to look a little embarrassed.

Emma sighed. Now what? Did she have to tell Darias about this? She didn't want to keep secrets from him, and this was exactly the kind of Jonas behavior she'd been afraid of when she—

"What's going on up here?" Darias's voice behind her made her spin around. His sister Lina was now halfway into her tight-fitting, lacy top.

"See if you can guess," said Jonas with a sneer.

"Jonas!" Rage flared in Emma's gut.

"Lina, what do you have to say for yourself?" Darias's shocked voice made his sister burst into tears, and she ran from the room, pushing past him on the way out. Darias strode up to Jonas, grabbed the front of his T-shirt and tugged him so hard she though he would lift off the floor.

Then he seemed to catch himself and instead turned and dashed out after his sister, calling her name.

Emma didn't know what to say. "Darias did a lot for you."

"And I'm clean, aren't I? I have to turn into a choirboy as well?"

She shook her head, feeling lost and adrift. "Don't say anything about this downstairs. Not unless someone else does. The less said the better."

"Sweep it under the rug, huh? Just like Mom."

"Don't say anything about Mom. She loved you and supported you to the end."

"Yeah." He sighed. "Some people just don't learn. Like you, for example."

"I told Darias not to invite you here." She said it as coldly as she could, even while her heart was breaking. "I knew something like this would happen. You're very predictable. I think you should leave as soon as possible."

He cocked his head. "You know what will happen."

"You'll start using again? After all this? I did this for you, Jonas. I do love you even though I think you're a total idiot most of the time."

"You did this for me?" His eyebrow lifted. He looked around the castle bedroom, then out the window, where there was a lovely view down over the town's slate roofs. "I was wondering about that. The timing intrigued me."

"What do you mean?" Fear spiked inside her.

"Won't they be wondering where you are?" He looked toward the door.

She glanced behind her, half wondering if the whole family might appear on the stairs, ready for revenge. "I suppose I'd better go down." Recrimination gnawed at her gut. "What are you going to do?"

"I'm going to come down, too, of course." He raked his hands through his hair, making it look artfully ruffled. "It would be rude not to. Besides, if you can marry Darias, why can't I date his sister? Have you thought about that?"

"It's different." She didn't want to say more. She was half beginning to wonder if he'd figured out their arrangement.

"I don't think so. It's not as if you're titled or wealthy or even successful and brilliant. You're just pretty. I'm handsome." He winked.

"You're an idiot."

"True. Shall we go downstairs?"

She let out a long, deep breath. Did she have any choice?

Emma dreaded coming upon some big scene as they exited the dim castle interior for the outside. Even the soft sunset seemed bright, and lanterns illuminated the space. The staff had rustled up an impromptu outdoor dinner, since no one seemed to want to leave.

Emma wished they hadn't. She'd breathe a lot easier if they all went home.

"Emma, darling, we thought we'd lost you," Darias's mom patted the empty chair she'd left earlier.

"Oh, I...." she had no idea what to say, so she didn't say anything. She looked around for Lina but didn't see her. Maybe she'd had the good sense to leave.

As soon as she sat down, Darias's mom leaned in. "Do you know what upset Lina? She was almost in tears. She rushed off."

Emma gulped. "Uh, I'm not sure. Would you like another drink?"

Liesel pulled up a chair, carrying a plate with two tiny pork ribs and a single candied carrot. "I suspect Lina was up to no good with that brother of yours." Her stage whisper could probably have been heard by anyone in the garden.

Emma opened her mouth, but no words came out.

"What were you thinking, to invite…" She turned and scowled at him, then turned back. "A *drug user* into our midst." She hissed the words *drug user* so dramatically it was a miracle a shower of spit didn't fly out.

"He's not using drugs," said Emma uselessly. "He was at a rehab facility and the treatment has worked really well and he…."

Her words trailed off as she noticed Darias's mom looking at Jonas in horror.

"I saw them sneaking off together when they thought no one was looking." Liesel looked smug. "What do you have to say for yourself, young man?" She dragged out the last two words as if they were actually curse words.

Jonas, far from looking sheepish or trying to run for the hills like Lina, helped himself to a piece of fresh bread and smeared some olive jam on it. After taking his time doing this, he finally looked up at Liesel. "She was asking for it. She's a college student. Did you think she was a virgin?"

Darias's mom, shocked, rose to her feet. "Your sister is the queen!" Her voice was barely above a shocked whisper. Beatriz watched with what looked like stunned amusement.

"Oh, my sister's always been the good one. I'm the black sheep of the family. I guess she didn't tell you that."

"Jonas!" Emma wished he'd hold his stupid tongue. Now he was just adding insult to injury.

"Oh!" He turned to her and made a mock bow to her, still holding his bread. "I'm so sorry, your majesty." He stopped and took a bite of bread, then spoke with his mouth full. "I wonder if your new royal relatives realize that Darias paid you to marry him."

Emma's blood froze.

How could he know?

"He *paid* her?" Liesel rose to her feet, grabbing her sister's arm as if to steady her.

Darias, who'd been standing off to the side presumably waiting for the fuss to die down, now strode in. "Where did you get that idea?"

"My sister," said Jonas insolently.

"I never said anything," burst Emma. After the words were out she realized they almost amounted to a confession. She glanced at Beatriz. Who winked at her.

"He *paid* you?" Liesel turned her beady blue eyes on Emma. "To marry him?"

Emma looked hopelessly at Darias. She didn't want to lie. How would that help matters?

Darias straightened his already broad shoulders. "Emma and I do have an…arrangement."

"What?" Darias's mom collapsed back in her

chair. "But I thought—" She looked at Emma, then Darias. A look of deep distress crossed her face.

"I knew that if I didn't find someone within the required thirty days, you would find someone for me." Darias's voice was uncharacteristically deep, even for him.

"Oh, those stupid traditions." Darias's mom waved a hand in the air. "I always thought there could be some small changes made to the constitution, but your father and grandmother always said that…" Her voice trailed off and she looked at Darias. "But you are…" She hesitated, sneaking a glance at Emma—who wished the ground would open up and swallow her. "You are in love, aren't you?"

Emma's heart started to pound. *Yes!* She wanted to cry. *I do love him. I love him so much it hurts.*

"No," said Darias softly. "I'd never met her until the day before I flew back here. It was a business arrangement, pure and simple. Sandro spotted her sitting at the desk in my New York gallery. The deal was made within hours."

He didn't look at her. She couldn't take her eyes off him. She'd signed a contract to keep their deal secret—from his family and the world—and now it was broken, their deception laid bare.

"And you chose, as your *wife*"—Liesel spat the word—"a nobody gallery assistant with a drug-addicted brother who has now cruelly seduced your youngest sister. Obviously you should have left matters up to your mother and myself."

Darias still hadn't looked at her. Every cell in Emma's body was telling her to run from the room. Not for the first time in her life, she wanted to kill Jonas—and now she rather wanted to wound Darias, too. Did he really think she'd told Jonas about their deal?

Her brother was being uncharacteristically silent. Wait—where was he? She scanned the smallish garden and didn't see him. Emma had been so caught up in the explosive release of her biggest secret, that she hadn't noticed him leave.

"Where's Jonas?" she blurted.

They all looked around. "Probably went after little Lina," muttered Liesel with a scowl.

He's probably gone looking for drugs. Emma felt a surge of fresh desperation rise in her chest. All this would truly be for nothing. "I'll go look for him."

"No, you stay here." Darias's voice was firm. "I'll go find him."

"Nonsense!" said Liesel, "Let the guards look for him. You don't need to—"

But Darias had already left the garden, striding back into the house.

"Oh, my goodness." Darias's mom looked pale and disoriented. "Just when I thought things were…"

"Shhh. Don't worry." Liesel sat down next to her and patted her arm. "We'll get everything sorted out eventually." Then Liesel pinned a steely gaze on Emma. "But first we need to get you out of here before the story breaks."

"What do you mean, out of here?" Maybe she should go hide in her room.

"Out of the castle. Out of Altaleone. Back to New York or New Jersey or wherever else you came from. You can go crawl back under your rock and leave us to pick up the pieces."

"But Darias said he needed to stay married for a year." They knew it all now, anyway.

Liesel gasped and looked around. "Did you hear how brazen she is? She admits it freely. What kind of girl can be bought for a year?"

A pretty stupid one, apparently. "I did it to help my brother." Her voice was barely audible.

"Who is now bringing shame to the house of Leone." Liesel shook her head. "You should never have invited him here."

I didn't. She wanted to say. *It was Darias's idea.* But blaming someone else would hardly make her look good.

"What's the problem anyway?" Chimed in Beatriz. "It's hardly different from a conventional arranged marriage. Just that there's a deadline at the end."

"An arranged marriage is invariably with a highly suitable girl of good family. I'm calling my travel agent." Liesel pulled a phone out of her pocket. "To get tickets for you and your brother on the first flight heading to New York."

Emma wanted to point out that a) it was nighttime b) she'd have to fly somewhere else first as there were no direct flights from Altaleone to New York c) travel agents were a thing of the past. But apparently Liesel got someone on the phone and barked at her in German for about two minutes, then hung up with a satisfied smile. "There's a shuttle to Vienna leaving tomorrow at ten, which connects to a flight to New York. Pack your bags, and I'll drive you to the airport myself."

"Hold on a moment." Darias's brother Sandro, who'd been watching the disaster unfold in the same stunned silence as everyone else, stood up. "Darias hasn't said that he wants her to leave. He made this arrangement. Let him handle it."

"Darias is the king," said Liesel. "His foremost responsibility is to the crown and the state of Altaleone."

"Which is exactly why he found and married Emma," protested Sandro. "It seems obvious to me that he did it to make old fusty traditionalists like you happy. We all like Emma very much." He turned to Emma. "Don't go. At least not without discussing any plans with Darias. He deserves that much."

She nodded. She'd had no intention of going anywhere. "Of course."

"Perhaps we should all leave Emma in peace," continued Sandro. "She's probably not really in the mood for entertaining."

She swallowed. Truer words had never been said.

"Your tickets will be at the Lufthansa counter." Liesel scrolled through a message on her phone, then rose with an arch look. "All the arrangements are made."

Emma nodded an insincere thanks. Should she use it?

No.

Darias's answer to the question about whether he loved her rang in her head like a tolled bell. Maybe it would be best for everyone if she did leave. Now they all had to keep the secret that their marriage was a pretense, a charade to keep up for one short year.

She pulled out her phone as they all left, punched up Darias's number and texted: **Did you find Jonas?**

Should I stay? That's what she really wanted to ask.

Yes. He was at The Ram, about to have a drink.

Exactly what she'd imagined. Jonas would throw everything she'd compromised herself for down the drain. And why shouldn't he? He hadn't asked her to sacrifice her integrity for him.

But don't worry, Darias wrote, **I stopped him**.

She sighed. Darias was effortlessly capable. Everything he tried led to success, from what she could see. If he could manage not to get killed by the mysterious assassins who'd murdered his forebears, he'd live long and prosper and forget all about her and their strange deal.

I'll come meet you, she replied.

She knew where The Ram was, right in the middle of the village, on the town square. She walked past the staff—now cleaning up the remains of their picnic using outdoor floodlights—and out into the street. It was odd, rather awesome really, that royals could just walk around the town like regular people.

Not that she was really royal, of course. Casteleone was one of the safest places on earth, partly because it was really tiny and everyone knew everyone else. Wrought iron lampposts held electric lanterns that cast picturesque shadows across the cobbled streets.

She turned away from the castle onto the tree-lined avenue leading to the main square, resolving not to put Darias on the spot about whether she should leave. This whole charade was his idea, and she'd wait to see what he suggested.

Hopefully, he wouldn't be too mad. Either way she'd try to be brave and—

A scented cloth closed over her mouth and a hard arm grabbed her around the waist, tugging her off her feet. She tried to scream, but the sound got lost in her throat as sudden blackness enveloped her.

23

"Wake up!" The words penetrated Emma's consciousness like a slap stung her cheek. *Female voice.* "I need proof that you're alive. Stop looking so dead."

Thoughts foggy, she couldn't make sense of the words. "Where am I?"

"Doesn't matter. Open your eyes."

Her mind fought against whatever they'd drugged her with. "Have I been kidnapped?

The woman's hollow laugh chilled her. "Yes, darling. Yes, you have."

"What do you want?"

"Information, that's all. From your *husband*." The sneering way she said the last word made Emma wonder if she knew their marriage was phony. Maybe they had found the missing contract.

Emma blinked against the light as her eyes cracked open. The woman wore a mask. A Cross of Blood mask, like the secret members had worn the night they'd come to the castle. Her gut clenched. Were they going to kill her? She didn't trust that group one bit.

"Your husband keeps texting you. He's getting worried."

"He's right to be worried," she murmured, trying to get a good look at the room. She lay on her back on the hard surface of a long table, her hands and feet tied to the legs with something. Bare plaster walls, no furniture except a nearly empty bookcase. No windows. Must be some kind of a basement. "What information do you want?"

"A number. You're going to call and ask him for it.

Emma recognized her voice from somewhere. She had a good ear for voices and remembered them much more easily than names or faces. She racked her mind, scrolling through people she'd met at the wedding, the coronation, until it dawned on her. This masked woman was Gemma, the one who had given Darias the gold cross but later turned out not to be a member of the Cross of Blood. What was she up to?

The woman held the phone up to her face. Unpainted nails and clean, soft hands. "When he answers, you're going to tell him you've been kidnapped, and you need to know the code for the Cross of Blood account."

"What makes you think there is one?"

She snorted. "None of your business. Ask him for it, then shut up while he says it. You can cry, though, or beg for mercy."

She heard the phone ring, then Darias answer, "Emma, where are you?"

"I've been kidnapped." She couldn't see any reason to keep that secret. "They want a number. A bank account code or something." She sounded strangely calm. Probably shock. Would he even believe her?"

"Where are you?" The tension in his voice told her instantly that he did believe her.

"I don't know. Some kind of basement." The woman snatched the phone away from her face and put it to her own. "The number now or she dies." She attempted to conceal her voice by rasping.

"I don't know what number you're talking about."

"Don't be stupid. I'm holding a gun to her head right now."

Emma wondered whether to yell, "She's not!" but decided that might actually get her killed. She was pretty sure there was another person in the room, and they might have a gun.

"Emma, are you okay?" She could hear Darias's voice even from far away.

"I am."

"Shut up." The woman smacked her across the mouth with her free hand. "The number now!"

"Um, hold on. Let me try to figure out which number you're talking about. I only just joined the Cross of Blood. Maybe I should call them and—"

He was stalling. Emma could tell. Darias always spoke directly, with few wasted words. Maybe Gibran was with him right now, tracing the location of the call.

"Don't call anyone." Gemma—Emma was now nearly 100 percent sure—forgot to conceal her voice. Then she cleared her throat and started rasping again. "You were given the code during the initiation."

"Was I? I don't remember that." Emma didn't remember it either, but then she hadn't heard the whole thing. "Maybe they decided to keep it secret. Is this why my father and grandmother died? Greed for money in some secret account they probably didn't know about either?"

She heard Darias's voice grow louder, even though the phone was several feet from her head.

"What is the number?" hissed Gemma.

"I told you, I'll have to find out. Hold on. I have an idea. Let me go look at…" Emma couldn't make out what he was saying. Or it didn't make any sense.

"Don't toy with me." Gemma forgot to disguise her voice again. She moved toward Emma and pinched her hard on the arm. She didn't cry out, so Gemma pulled her hair with vicious strength until an involuntary squeal left her mouth.

Gemma stared right at her, still tugging hard on her hair. "Am I hurting you, Emma?"

"Y…yes."

"See, Darias? You need to pay attention. The number now! I'm going to call back in two minutes and you need to give it to me or you're going to hear your wife die over the phone."

She hung up. "Shit, I wonder if he's tracing the call. I felt like he was just dragging it out."

"He's probably already given his phone to the chief of security." Emma felt strangely calm and brave herself. At least Darias wasn't here to get hurt or killed.

"Shut up." She dropped her hair and smacked her again, making her cheek sting. "If he comes with anyone, we'll kill you. You need to tell him that when we call back."

Horror tightened Emma's gut. The words that

emerged in her mind were a mix of self-preservation and the ugly truth. "You can go ahead and kill me. He wouldn't care."

"What?" A male voice. From behind her head where she couldn't see him. "Why not?"

"He doesn't love me." Maybe if she could convince them she was useless, they'd let her go without involving Darias. She didn't want him to come here and end up dead, like his relatives.

Should she keep what was left of their secret or spill it to try to save them both?

"He only married me because he had to. We barely know each other. We already have plans to part after a year."

The male let out a string of curses.

"She's bluffing." The girl again. "It's nonsense. I've known him long enough to tell when he's serious about something."

If only that were true.

"Are you sure your greed hasn't blinded you? If your plans made any sense we'd have got the code from the old lady. I've done everything you asked, and we still don't have it."

"We will. Stay calm. He was initiated into the Cross of Blood so he knows the code. All we have to do is get it out of him."

"We could have just sold the damn cross when we had it. But no! You had to give it back to him into a dramatic gesture." The young man's voice grew whiny.

"You can't fence something like that. It would have to be melted down and go for a fraction of its value. I only got it because I hoped the code was in it or on it somewhere. Focus on what we're doing." She hissed the last words angrily.

"But if he doesn't give a rat's ass about her…" His voice spat the last word in Emma's direction. "He won't come and he won't tell us the number."

"Trust me."

"I've done everything you asked and look where the hell we are." His voice was rough with desperation.

"I didn't tell you to throw that stupid firework. What the hell were you thinking?"

"I got him to join the Cross of Blood, didn't I?"

While they argued back and forth, Emma focused intently on the strips of fabric—bandages, maybe?—binding her hands and feet to the table. It was slightly stretchy, so if she could manage to move a hand or foot enough, without it being visible, of course, she might be able to—

"Stop moving!" The woman's hand slapped her across the face again. Her cheek smarted from the repeated blows. Then she pulled up Emma's phone. "It's time to call him again. Just tell him to say the code or you die right now." She punched in his number, then held the phone up to Emma's face.

Blinking, Emma heard it ring. Her gut clenched as Darias's low voice answered. "I know what code you're talking about, but I have to go get it."

"Be careful, Darias. They're armed." She had a gut feeling he was on his way here.

Gemma snatched the phone away. "The code, this instant, or she's dead."

"Gemma, is that you?" Emma heard Darias's words.

Gemma panicked and hung up the phone. "Shit!" Emma could only see her out of the corner of her eye, from where she lay on the table. "He knows it's me."

"Why did you hang up? How can he give you the code? Give the phone to me." The young man wrenched it rudely from her. He punched something, and she heard Darias answer immediately and ask, "Where are you?"

"Darias—if you don't give me the code right now, your queen gets a bullet in her brain." She heard a click and cold metal pushed against her temple.

She couldn't stop a panicked whimper. The man, also masked, pushed it against her head harder. "Tell him I'm serious."

"He has a gun...." Her voice was a shaky whisper. She tried to sound louder. "A gun pressed to my head."

"If you injure one hair on her head you will die today." She heard Darias's steely voice through the phone.

"Idle threats. You don't know where I am."

"That's what you think."

BOOM. Something pounded hard against the door. "What the—?" Her two assailants stood frozen for a second, then the man pulled the gun from her head, aimed it at the door and fired. The loud sound and the crunch of the bullet hitting the door made Emma scream. "Darias, he's armed. Don't come in."

With a loud crunching sound, the heavy wood door exploded out of its doorway, and Gibran ploughed in over it and fired a bullet right into the armed man, hitting his arm, which dropped the gun.

Gemma reached for the fallen gun, but a guard launched from behind Gibran and pinned her to the floor, then another guard pushed the injured kidnapper to the floor. Emma fought against her bonds, cries for help pealing from her mouth even though she knew she should wait.

Darias crashed in from behind Gibran. "Thank God you're okay." The sight of him sent relief and waves of panic and joy pouring through her. He tugged at the bandages binding her left hand, then pulled a Swiss army knife from his pocket and slit them all. In seconds she was in his arms, pulled tight against his chest.

Her heart beat furiously as emotion swept through her. "I didn't want you to come. They might have tried to kill you. I think they killed your father and grandmother because they wouldn't give them a secret code from the Cross of Blood." She spewed it out in a jumbled rush, wanting him to know that these were the murderers.

"We didn't kill them," Gemma protested. "We never killed anyone. We just want the money." She was handcuffed and being led out by Gibran's men. Her accomplice had already left, a trail of blood following him from his wounded arm.

"We'll let the law figure that out."

"What day is it? Have I missed my plane?" She didn't want him to think that she imagined this somehow let her off the hook. She lowered her voice. "I told them about...you know." She glanced at Gibran and the men, who probably still didn't know that their marriage was a sham. Or maybe everyone knew by now. It might have leaked out if the family members were talking.

Darias's face hardened, and he pulled back from her and inhaled. She braced herself for whatever he might say. "Emma Leone, I'm ashamed of myself for even thinking I could do such a thing. What kind of man asks a warm, kind and loving woman to sell her soul for a year?"

She swallowed. What kind of woman would agree? He must think very little of her now.

"And then bed her, to boot? What kind of a man does that?" He shook his head, dark eyes gleaming with…something. "I don't know if I can ever forgive myself."

"It's okay. I shouldn't have said yes, but I did." Her heart was breaking. Darias would send her away. Neither of them should ever have embarked on such a deceitful course. Lying to his closest relatives, the people of Altaleone and the entire world. Now the truth was out he felt rightfully embarrassed—ashamed—by what he'd done. He would make amends. Maybe give her more money to hide herself away with and—

"I deserve to be horsewhipped for even coming up with such a despicable plan."

She wanted to point out that it was actually Sandro's idea, but that probably wouldn't help anyone. "You did it for your mom," she said. "And I did it for my brother. We didn't want to hurt anyone." She already forgave herself. Yes, the aftermath would hurt like heck, but she'd get through it.

Darias nodded, sudden tears glittered in his eyes. Was he thinking about how devastated his mom was by the crushing news that it was all fake?

"Emma Leone. I wish our marriage had started in truth and honesty, and with all the love and honor that I intend to shower on you for the rest of our lives together."

What?

Face taut with emotion, he continued. "I love you with every ounce of my being. I love you in ways I never dreamed myself capable of loving anyone. I love you so much that living without you would drive me insane. I know you can never love me after the way I've used you, then seduced you. I don't ask for your love. But I promise you from this day on I will do the best I can to be a kind and loving and loyal and truly faithful husband to you if you'll only agree to stay with me, and perhaps in time you can grow to love me the way people did in the old days when they were forced into arranged marriages."

Emma's brain was spinning so fast she could hardly made sense of his words. *He loved her and didn't think she loved him?* It seemed impossible.

She had been so, so careful never to let him know that she loved him. So sure that it would upset him or drive him away.

A tear did roll down over his hard cheek as he got down on one knee. "I never did propose to you, Emma. Not in any way a decent man would propose. But if you would do me the honor of being my wife, I'd be the happiest man alive."

She couldn't find words. "I'm already your wife."

"Legally, yes. But one day, with enough time, I hope to win your heart and make you truly mine."

A sob rose in her throat. *Did he really not know that*

she loved him? "I love you." The words emerged as a choked whisper.

"I know I don't deserve a woman as good as you, but on my honor I will try my best to become a husband worthy of you, if you'll only agree to stay with me."

"I love you." This time she managed to make the words more audible. "I do want to stay with you." She could hardly believe this. Maybe she'd been knocked unconscious by the kidnappers, and this was some kind of feverish fantasy taking place in her injured brain. She used a recently freed hand to pinch herself.

I'm awake.

"Did you say you love me?" Darias looked stunned.

"Yes. I do love you. I've loved you for weeks now."

He blinked. "All this time, and you never—?" He frowned. "Why would you say anything to me? I was being an ass. Trying to preserve my *freedom*"—he spat the word—"illusory freedom that means nothing to me."

He took her hands and held them tight, then drew them to his mouth and kissed her fingers. "I don't want to be free, of either my duty to my country or my marriage to you. I love you so much, Emma Leone."

Tears fell so hard and fast that she couldn't even see his expression. He took her in his arms and kissed her, and she kissed him back even harder and they embraced and held each other until her tears started to slow.

A man cleared his throat.

They both looked up. "If you'll excuse me, sir." It was Gibran. "The prisoners will be taken in for questioning. His wound will be treated, of course."

"They're likely the murderers, no matter what they say," said Darias, showing far more presence of mind than Emma still had.

"Indeed. They will be treated as such." Then a smile creased Gibran's stern, sun-weathered face. "Congratulations, sir."

Darias grinned. "Much appreciated."

Back at the castle, a small group of reporters had already gathered outside in the dark as they walked in, flanked by security. "Did you catch the murderers?" "Will they be hanged?" "Is it true that she's a bride for hire?"

Emma cringed under the last question. How did word get out so quickly? Was every word they said being recorded and leaked somehow? Or was it someone inside the family?

Darias stopped and turned to face them. "This woman is the love of my life. Our marriage may have started out as a convenient arrangement like those of my ancestors, but I promise you that no man—king or otherwise—ever loved a woman more than I love Emma." His soft kiss on her cheek led to a flurry of camera clicks and flashes, and a hot surge of emotion that threatened to choke her.

Still, Emma was self-conscious enough to hope she didn't look too awful after having her face slapped repeatedly.

"And do you love him, too, miss?" one older

reporter called.

"I do." She smiled at Darias.

He grabbed her hand and pulled her toward the castle doors. "They'll keep us out here all night if we let them, and I can't have that happen. I have my own plans for you."

They showered together, soaping and caressing each other, unafraid of their own desire and with nothing to hide. Then they made love with passion and intensity she would never have dared to express before tonight.

"I love you," she breathed at the moment of release, thrilled that she could finally say the words dancing on the tip of her tongue for weeks.

"I love you, too, Mrs. Leone." Darias nuzzled her cheek. "I think I started loving you the first night we met, but I'm very slow on the uptake sometimes."

"Probably all the royal inbreeding," she teased.

"No doubt." He nibbled her ear gently, sparking a rush of arousal. "All the more reason to marry a sexy commoner from New Jersey."

"You can pretend you planned it that way all along."

"No way." He pulled back enough to gaze at her with a look that stole her breath. "No more pretense, no more lies. We'll tell the truth and let everyone enjoy—or laugh at—the king whose best-laid plans to stay single led to him falling head over heels in love."

THE END

The complete Royal House of Leone Series:
The King's Bought Bride (Darias and Emma)
A Prince for Christmas (Sandro and Serena)
The Prince's Secret Baby (Sandro and Serena)
The Princess and the Player (Lina and Amadou)
The Princess's Scandalous Affair (Beatriz and Lorenzo)
Taming the Royal Beast (Rigo and Bella)

Join the new-release newsletter at www.jenlewis.com.

ABOUT THE AUTHOR

Jennifer Lewis loves heat in all its forms including spicy food, steamy temperatures and smoking hot heroes. She is a USA TODAY bestselling author and her books have been translated into more than twenty languages. She lives in sunny South Florida and when she's not sitting at her laptop she can often be found at the beach. Read more about her books and join her new release mailing list at www.jenlewis.com.